A Damsel in Distress?

"Hello," I managed to gasp out. "Were you talking to me?"

"Yes," said the yellow-haired girl. "I was. Help me down from here. I'm locked in."

"Princesses locked in towers!" cried Laura enthusiastically. "I knew this was going to be an adventure! Is a wicked ogre holding you prisoner? Does he beat you and feed you on bread and water?"

"Why, yes," said the yellow-haired girl. "That's exactly what he does!" And then she clasped her hands and looked straight at me. "Save me, gallant knight!" she cried. "Take me with you on your noble steed before the wicked ogre returns!"

"All right," I said.

But as I studied the castle, I wasn't sure how I was going to do it. Roses wreathed the stones of the tower romantically, but their stems looked frail for climbing, and thorny besides. And the girl's hair, while ample and suitably golden, was not of Rapunzel length.

"Just a minute," I said. "I'll think of something."

"There's a ladder in the barn," said the girl, rather impatiently, I thought. "Hurry!"

THE
WELL-WISHERS

THE
WELL-WISHERS

EDWARD EAGER

ILLUSTRATED BY N. M. BODECKER

HOUGHTON MIFFLIN HARCOURT

Boston   New York

First Harcourt Young Classics edition 1999
First Odyssey Classics edition 1990
First published 1960

The Library of Congress has cataloged the hardcover edition as follows:
Eager, Edward.
The well-wishers/by Edward Eager; illustrated by N. M. Bodecker.
p. cm.
Sequel to: Magic or not?
Summary: James, Laura, and Deborah, along with their friends
Kip, Lydia, and Gordy, relate their experiences when the
unpredictable old wishing well in the backyard continues
to involve them in a series of magical adventures.
[1. Magic—Fiction. 2. Wishes—Fiction.
3. Interpersonal relations—Fiction.]
I. Bodecker, N. M., ill. II. Title.
PZ7.E115We 1999
[Fic]—dc21 99-22564

ISBN: 978-0-544-67167-6 paperback

Printed in the United States of America
DOC 10 9 8 7 6 5 4 3
4500707321

*For all my friends and relations
named Stephen and Michael*

Contents

1
James Begins

I know people who say they can read any kind of book except an "I" book, and sometimes I think I agree with them. When I say "I" books, I mean the kind where somebody tells the story, and it starts out, "Little did I think when I first saw the red house how large it would loom in my life." And later on, the person sees a sinister stranger digging a grave in the garden and he says, "If I had only remembered to telephone the police next morning, seven murders might have been averted."

Laura and I often run into books like that, and Laura always says she holds the people who tell those stories in utter contempt, which is her way of saying they give her a pain. If we saw a sinister stranger digging a grave in our garden, we would remember to telephone the police, all right. And when we first saw *our* red house, we *knew* how large it would loom.

Laura is my sister, and not bad as sisters go. Sometimes she has quite sound ideas.

One of her ideas was that we should tell the story this way, "I" book or not. Because the things that happened that winter happened to six of us (not counting parents), and the way they happened was different for each person. The way we felt about it was different for each person, too. So it is only right that each one should tell his part.

Laura says I should begin the whole thing because I have a well-organized mind. I am not boasting. That about my mind is what Mrs. Van Nest said one day. Mrs. Van Nest is our teacher, and sometimes her ideas are quite sound, too. She lets us do book reports on any book we like, and it doesn't have to be on the list.

So I am beginning this story, and after that each one will tell what happened to him or her, as the case may be, and each one will tell it in his own way. Only we have made one rule, which is not to tell about the days when nothing happened, because who would want to read about them? And another rule is not to put in things that don't mean anything and are just there to try to make it more exciting. Like saying, "There I stood, my heart beating." Naturally your heart would be beating. Otherwise you wouldn't be standing there; you'd be lying down dead.

But we are going to stick to the facts.

The first important fact about me is that my name is James Alexander Martin and I am in grade six-one-A, Mrs. Van Nest's homeroom. Kip and Laura and Lydia are all in my class, too, but Gordy is in six-one-B and has to have Miss Wilson. Wow, do I pity him!

We try to be specially kind to Gordy, for that and other reasons, but sometimes we forget. Gordy is not a person who makes it easy for other people always to remember. Sometimes we have to be firm with him for his own good, but we try never to stoop to physical violence. Physical violence never solved anything in the world, we all realize. But sometimes with Gordy we forget that, too, or at least Kip and I do. Girls are soft.

If you wonder why Laura and I are in the same class in school, it is because we are the same age, being twins. But we do not look alike, or think alike, either, particularly about the magic, only that comes later.

As for my other sister Deborah, she is a mere babe, just starting the first grade, and by rights she shouldn't come into this story at all. But rights have never meant a great deal to Deborah.

The story I'm talking about began one day in fall.

Of course it really began long before that, way back at the beginning of the summer, when Laura and I and our family first moved into the red house on Silvermine Road. Before that we lived in New York City.

The red house has a well in the garden, and the day we moved in a girl called Lydia Green, who lives in a funny big old place up the road, told us that it was a wishing well. Of course I knew better than to believe that. But Laura would believe anything, or try to.

Still, some very strange things did happen that summer. A lot of quite good wishes came true and some pretty keen good turns got done. That was the way the well was supposed to work. Selfish wishes didn't mean a thing to it.

We got our heart's desire in the end, too, just like in that book *The Wonderful Garden* by E. Nesbit that Laura is so crazy about. It is not a bad book, by the way. A boy runs away and so does a tiger, and a portrait comes to life. The ending is nifty, if you're young enough to believe in magic.

I'm not sure whether I am young enough or not. Mostly I think not. Magic doesn't seem at all like the kind of thing that *would* be true, when you come to think of it. Still, neither do airplanes and electric lights and outer space, when you come to think of *them*. And it's hard to explain the things that happened that summer any other way. Or the things that have been happening since, either. Of course it may all be a coincidence, the way Kip keeps saying.

Kip is a boy called Christopher, only he never is. Never is called that, I mean. He lives on our road, too, across from Lydia. He is a good kid, and just about my best friend, I guess.

He and Lydia and Laura and I were in on the magic (if that's what it was) from the beginning. Gordy didn't come into it till later in the summer. We didn't *ask* him in exactly, but once he was there, we didn't mind. Sometimes his ideas are every bit as sound as ours. All he needs is to be curbed once in a while, and shoved back on the right road. He is the victim of an unfortunate environment. His mother is rich. His full name is Gordon T. Witherspoon III.

When we first made the wish about our heart's desire, we weren't quite sure what our heart's desire was, but when we got it, we knew. What it turned

5

out to be was a little old house in the woods, all our own, to have for our secret clubhouse. How we found the house in the first place, and what we found in it, and exactly how it got to be ours is another story, and if you want to read that story, you will have to get a book called *Magic or Not?* that tells all about it. But we did not write that book ourselves; so it does not have all our thoughts in it, the way this book will.

The part about the heart's desire came right at the end of the summer, and after that the magic (if it *was* magic) seemed to be played out. At least we made quite a few perfectly good wishes on the well and they never came true, no matter how noble. That was all right with me, if that was how the well wanted things to end. But the girls said it was probably just resting and would start up again one day when we least expected it. You never can tell with magic. Or not, as the case may be.

And then suddenly it was fall, and for Laura and me there was a new school to get used to, and learning a new teacher's ways and how to circumscribe them, if that is the word I mean, and that took up all our thoughts, for a while.

Football season began, too; so Kip and I were

mainly too busy to bother with girls. I play end, but not very often, being light though rangy. Baseball is my game.

Laura and Lydia do not understand the true importance of football, or baseball either, but that is their female folly. As you grow older, the sexes grow farther and farther apart, I find. It is all part of maturing.

Still, the old group did find time to meet now and then in the house in the woods and have secret conclaves, though there wasn't very much to conclave *for,* now that the magic was a thing of the past.

Maybe that's how we got into the habit of leaving Gordy out; so we'd have something to be secret about. We even had a mysterious secret sign. When it seemed like a good day for a meeting, one of us would hold up one finger, or two, along toward the end of last period. One if all five, two if without Gordy. Lately it was getting to be two most of the time.

Sometimes Gordy would come into the woods looking for us, but when he found us in the secret clubhouse without him, he never seemed to bear any grudge. That is one of the good things about Gordy.

We were always sorry afterward when this happened, and the fact that Gordy didn't seem to get hurt or mad at us made us feel sorrier. You would think that would make us be nicer to him from then on, but it didn't. The sorrier we felt each time, the more we went on leaving him out the next. That is the way people are. I do not think this is right, but it is true all the same. Though unfortunate.

This particular day Kip had held up two fingers just as the last bell rang, and we had all nodded, and when we marched out, everybody but Lydia got away quick without being spotted by the enemy. And Lydia crossed her fingers and told Gordy she had to go to the dentist. Which was not a lie really, because she *did* have to go. Only not that day.

So now there we all were (except you know whom) sitting on the front stoop of the secret house, because it was getting to be late September and the rooms inside were cold. But in front, the woods have been cut away to let the sun through.

Lydia had a pencil in her hand and a sketchbook in her lap, the way she does all the time now that she knows she has talent. It is wonderful how learning that she has talent has changed that girl. Maybe learning to make friends has had something to do with it, too. When we first met her, she was plain ornery, always doing crazy things just to be different, and quarreling with everybody. She is still ornery once in a while, and she and I still argue some. But she is a good kid, for a girl.

Today she was amusing us by doing caricatures of each one. The ones she did of Laura and Kip were awfully funny, but she didn't get me right at all. My chin doesn't stick out like that, at least not that far.

When we'd finished arguing about my chin, she started a portrait of herself, all long tangled blond hair with a scowl peeking through. Then she made a face at it and tore it up. "If you ask me," she said, "it's time something started happening around here. I'm used to school again. The sameness has set in."

"Halloween next month," Kip reminded her. "There's the party in the gym."

"Bobbing for apples!" Lydia was scornful. "And that old decoration committee. Black crepe paper cats on the walls; you'd think they could at least think up something original. Why didn't they put *me* on it; *I'd* freeze their marrow for them!" And she drew a truly horrendous witch on the next page of her sketch pad.

"If you ask *me*," said Laura, "I think the trouble with us is we miss the magic."

Everybody groaned, because we were all secretly trying not to think about that. But Laura is a great one for bringing hidden thoughts out into the open.

"We said this was going to be our secret witches' den where we'd have midnight meetings and plan our secret spells," she went on now. "We were going to do good turns to the whole town. But not a single magic thing's happened, and pretty soon it'll be too cold to come here anymore."

"It'll be warm again in the spring," I said. "Maybe

the magic goes to sleep in the winter, like wood-chucks."

"In books it's almost always summer when the magic starts working," put in Kip. "It's almost always summer vacation."

"So we won't be distracted from our lessons, I suppose," said Lydia bitterly. "As if being distracted weren't just what we need!"

"Has anybody said anything to the well lately?" I wondered. "Maybe it's just sitting there waiting for a friendly word." After all, if we were going to believe in the magic (and everyone was talking suddenly as if we were), we might as well be efficient about it.

"No, and I don't think we ought to," said Laura. "I think we're supposed to wait, no matter how long it takes."

"Then let's not talk about it," I said. Because there is nothing so maddening as talking about something when you can't do a single thing about it.

"I think we *ought* to talk," said Laura. "I think we've been silent about it, and each going his own way, long enough." She turned to Lydia. "You didn't say a thing when James asked if anybody'd been talk-ing to the well lately, and neither did Kip. Have you been wishing on the sly?"

"I did think of giving it a look and a few words the other day," Lydia admitted. "Just sort of generally about getting a move on. But I thought better of it."

"I almost asked it to help with my history test," said Kip. "And that would have been unselfish, because think how my parents would feel if I flunked. I didn't do it, though. Maybe I should have. I only got a seventy-one."

"No," said Laura. "I think it's a good thing you didn't. I think if we start pestering it, it might get cross and take longer waking up than it would have, even. Or go all wrong when it does. I think we ought to swear a secret oath in blood not to go *near* the well until we're absolutely sure it's time."

Everybody was willing, probably because even merely swearing a secret oath is *sort* of a secret adventure. Kip had his scout knife handy, pricks were made, and the fatal oath duly sworn.

"There," said Laura, sucking a finger. "That's settled. Now when the well's ready, it'll tell us so. There'll be a sign."

"What kind of a sign?" Kip wondered. "Will it go guggle guggle guggle? Or shoot up like a geyser?"

"Something'll happen," said Laura. "We'll know."

There was a sound in the woods.

Everybody jumped. But it wasn't the kind of sound magic would make starting up at all. It was a crackling and a swishing and a thudding that could add up to only one thing: Gordy.

When Gordy runs through the woods, branches don't mean a thing to him, or noise either. As a Commando, his name would be mud. He does get where he's going, though. And he does not seem to mind the scratches.

We could hear his voice now, high and kind of bleating the way it always is, and mingled with a childish prattle. At the sound of the prattle, the words "Oh help" rose to the lips of many.

Because fond as we are of my little sister Deborah, at a secret meeting she can be a menace. But Gordy has no sense of the fitness of things. And he indulges Deborah in her whims, and this is bad for her character.

Sure enough, when he came trotting into the clearing, we saw that he was giving Deborah a piggyback ride, a thing no one must ever do, because once you give in to her, she wants to do it all the time. They came up onto the stoop, Gordy breathing hard and forgetting to close his mouth. But I must not make personal remarks. We all have our bad habits. Lydia used to bite her nails and I drum with my fingers.

"Hi," he said, putting Deborah down and beaming round at us. "What are you all doing? Huh?"

And right away we all got the feeling we always do when we've run away from Gordy and then he follows us and finds us.

It's partly a guilty feeling, and part embarrassed and part really sorry, too. Because we like Gordy. We honestly do. Nobody could help it. It's just that there is something about him that makes people want to pick on him. You have heard of people who are accident prone. Gordy is picking-on prone.

"Gordy rode me all the way here on his handlebars and then piggybacked me through the woods. Wasn't that *kind?*" said Deborah.

And of course it was. Gordy is just as kind as he can be. And he and Deborah get along like all get out, maybe because their childish minds meet and mingle. "Gordy said maybe you'd rather be by yourselves without him for a change, but I told him that was silly," Deborah was saying now.

Everybody stirred uncomfortably.

"I just love Gordy," she went on. "Don't you?" Sometimes I think she says the things she does on purpose.

"Sure, he's a good kid," Kip muttered.

Gordy hung his head and said, "Aw."

In another second I think the guilty feeling would have exploded and we might have started pushing Gordy around, just in a friendly way, and probably all joined in some childish scuffle, which is the best way to get rid of feelings.

If only Deborah had kept her mouth shut. But that is a thing she finds it impossible to do, apparently, now she is in the first grade and has learned to read. Last summer we could hardly get a word out of her.

"We're going to have magic wishes all the time from now on," she babbled happily. "Gordy's fixed the well."

There was a sound of a breath being caught and held and everyone looked at Laura. She had gone perfectly white. "What?" she said. But it did not sound like her voice talking.

"Gordy's fixed the well," repeated Deborah. "He went right up to it and told it what."

"Oh," said Laura.

Maybe I should explain right here that usually my

sister Laura is the most decent and reasonable of all of us, but on the subject of the well she is different. Sometimes you would think it was her own special private property. Maybe that is because she is the one who started the wishes working in the first place.

She turned to Gordy. "All right, Gordy Witherspoon," she said. "What have you done *now?*"

Personally I consider "What have you done *now?*" a perfectly awful question. If anybody said, "What have you done *now?*" to me, it would make me think of all the things I had done before and I would know they had all been bad and this new thing was the worst, and that everybody hated me and I might as well go out in the garden and eat worms. But Gordy did not seem to mind.

"Oh nothing," he said. "I just tossed a wish down."

"He wrote it all out," said Deborah proudly, "on the back of my spelling paper. I got a hundred. And a gold star." Only nobody was listening because we were all watching Laura.

But "What did the wish say?" was all she asked. It was the way she said it that counted.

"Oh, nothing," Gordy said again. "I don't remember. Yes I do, too. I told it, 'Get going, or else. This means you.'"

For a minute I thought Laura was going to hit him.

I decided it was time to speak up. "Let's not get excited," I started to say. "Maybe that was a little crude."

"Crude?" Laura interrupted. "Crude? It just doesn't show even the first ruminants of good taste, that's all!"

"OK," I said. "Maybe it doesn't. But that's still not a crime or anything. Gordy didn't know about the oath. He was just trying to please Deborah. And we've all been ruder than that to the well in our day."

"That's different," said Laura. "The magic *belongs* to us. It doesn't to him." She turned on Gordy again. "You've just ruined everything utterly and completely, Gordy Witherspoon, and I hope you're satisfied." And then she said words I never expected to hear from a sister of mine. "You always were a buttinski and a pest and we never wanted you around in the first place, and now you can just go on home and never come back!"

This was too much for me. "Here, wait a minute," I said, getting up and coming between them.

And even Kip, who is usually too lazy and easygoing to move, uncurled himself from the floor and went and put an arm round Gordy's shoulder, though we all hate sloppiness and what the books call "demonstrations of affection."

Because while it is perfectly true that we have roughed Gordy up once in a while when he needed it, and Kip *did* give him a bloody nose one day (though he got a black eye for it), and one other time when Gordy was really awful I *may* have put him across my knee and spanked him, just once or twice to help him grow up; still, neither of us would ever have spoken to a fellow human being like that. Sticks and stones may break your bones, but names and plain truths and meanness can go much deeper and cut you to the quick. We know this, and Laura knows it, too, when she is in her right mind.

But sometimes I think that Gordy does not have any quick. For he went right on smiling. Though maybe his voice did sound a little higher and more bleating than usual.

"I'm sorry," he said. "I didn't mean to butt in. I just thought it was time somebody did something, and you were afraid to. And Deborah wanted the wishes to start over, so I thought why not try?"

There's one thing you can say for Gordy, he is spunky. I was sure that word "afraid" would be the last straw that would send Laura through the needle's eye into utter frenzy. But maybe she thought she had said enough already. For she didn't answer a word, but turned and went into the cold, dark, empty house, as if she wanted to be by herself. Gordy hesitated a minute, and then he went in after her. He certainly has spunk, all right.

Of course it would have been tactful, and better manners, to have left them to settle it on their own. But manners have never stopped Deborah. She followed Gordy right in. After that, the rest of us were too curious to be behindhand.

And besides, I wasn't sure it was safe for Gordy to be alone with Laura, in the mood she was in.

But when we came into the secret house's tiny parlor, Laura wasn't doing a thing, just standing with her back to the room, looking down at the desk in one corner (the desk that was such a big part of our adventure the summer before) and fiddling with the key, moving it back and forth in the lock. Gordy went right up to her and took her by the shoulders and turned her round. He held out his hand.

"I'm sorry, honest," he said. "I guess I just don't know any better."

Nobody could have said it straighter. When I thought of what Laura had just said to *him,* I thought

20

it was pretty big. And Deborah ran right up to Gordy and put her arm around his waist, which is as high up on him as she can reach.

Laura was looking at the floor. But what we could see of her face wasn't white anymore. It was red. She hesitated. And then I'm glad to say she took Gordy's hand, kind of grabbing at it and dropping it right away, but not as if she didn't like him. More as if she didn't like herself.

"I'm sorry, too," she said.

"Oh, that's all right," Gordy said.

"I didn't really mean all that," she said.

"Sure. Of course you didn't," Gordy said.

"It'd be awful if I did. The magic's supposed to be for doing good turns. It'd be awful if just thinking about it could make me say a thing like that and mean it."

"But you *didn't* mean it," Gordy said.

"That's right, I didn't. It's just that . . ." Her voice trailed off and I thought it was time for me to step in again.

"What Laura means," I said, "is that she was forgetting you don't know about magic, much, yet. She was forgetting you just came in at the end of it, last summer. You see, magic has rules, the same as anything else. If you talk to it the way you did and begin ordering it around, there's no telling what it might do. If the well starts up again now, and if it's angry and goes wrong, it'll be your fault and you'll just have to bear the brunt and take the consequences."

Laura stamped her foot. "No, silly! That's not what I meant at all!"

"Isn't it?" I said. But I was pleased.

"No, it isn't." And now she sounded like the old Laura again. "We can't blame Gordy. He didn't know. If it goes wrong, we're all in it together, naturally. But if everything's all right and it turns out to be a *good* adventure, I think he ought to be in charge of the whole thing. Because he had the courage to really speak up to the well and get it going."

That shows you what kind of girl my sister is. Particularly when everyone knew she had had dibs on the first wish right along.

It was Gordy's face that was red now. "Aw no, you ought to be the one. Honest, I'd rather."

Laura shook her head. "This is the only way it'd be fair."

"How do you mean, be in charge?" Gordy said cautiously. "You'd all be along, wouldn't you? You'd be in the adventure, too? It wouldn't be any fun, otherwise."

"Oh sure, we'd all be along," Laura told him. "If the magic starts, we'll be there and help out any way we can. But you'll be the one to make the decisions."

Everybody else nodded. Personally I thought it was giving Gordy a lot of rope. Still, maybe it would turn out to be just what he needed to make a man of him. So I nodded, too.

Gordy looked awed. "Gee," he said. "I don't know if I'm up to it."

"Sure you are," said Laura.

"Sure you are," repeated Deborah.

Gordy looked down at her. They smiled at each other. Then he grinned at the rest of us. "All right," he said. "I'll try."

There was a silence.

And then, in the silence, we all heard a knock at the front door.

Everybody looked at everybody else. And there wasn't a doubt in anybody's mind that the magic was beginning again right now.

Because nobody ever knocks at the door of the secret house.

Our parents and our friends and relations know that it *is* secret, and that is its charm, and they wouldn't dream of ever coming near it and disturbing us. And besides it's too hard a walk for most parents, through the woods and all uphill. Or downhill, if you come from behind. If we're at the secret house and a friend or a relation wants us, he stays at the foot of the hill, by the road, and rings. We have a system, made of wires and pulleys and an old cowbell.

So if somebody had come knocking at our front door on this cold September afternoon, with the sun going down and everything getting dark, it stood to reason that only the magic could have sent him.

The knock came again.

Laura grinned at Gordy. "It's all yours," she said.

Gordy gulped. "Gee," he said. Then he went into the hall and opened the front door.

And now it's his turn to tell what happened next.

2

Gordy Tries

This is Gordy telling the story now.

I went into the hall and opened the front door, but I was not as calm as that makes me sound. I was scared.

I am really scared a lot of the time. Not just of spooky, mysterious knockings on doors, but of ordinary things like meeting people and wondering what they will think of me. That's why I say loud dumb things sometimes, to cover up how scared I am. I can hear exactly how loud and dumb they are, right while I'm saying them. But it is too late then.

I try never to let James and Kip and Laura and Lydia see how scared I am, though. They would despise me if they knew. They aren't scared of anything. So I went into the hall and opened the front door.

But when I saw the figure that was standing there, I almost shut it again. And Deborah, who was following me, took one look at the figure, and screamed out "Witches!" and ran back into the parlor.

"Eh?" said the figure in the doorway, leaning forward and cupping its ear with one hand. "What was that?"

"Oh, nothing," I said. "How do you do?" I added. That was all I could think of. And then I probably just stood there with my mouth hanging open. I know I do that sometimes.

The figure was female, but that's about all you could say for it. I have heard some people claim that Lydia's grandmother, old Mrs. Green the artist, goes around looking like a witch. All I can say is, compared with this old lady, Lydia's grandmother is Marlene Dietrich.

This old lady was all huddled into a long black cloak, and her straggly white hair was coming half down and blowing in the wind. To make her all the more witchlike, her gnarly knotty hands were full of leafy branches and plant stalks and long pieces of vine that trailed down to the ground. She wore big horn-rimmed spectacles and her nose was long and thin and her fingers were long and thin, and when she grinned, it was exactly like a crocodile.

She grinned now. And she pointed one of her long thin fingers straight at me.

"Young man," she said in a cracked voice, "I seem to have lost my way. Can you direct me to Hopeful Hill?"

At these words my heart sank. And I was sure I had started the magic and it was cross as two sticks about it, and I was doomed.

To know why, you would have to know about Hopeful Hill.

It is on our road, and some people say it is a crazy house and call it Hopeless Hill. This is not true. Not exactly.

It is a place where unhappy people come for the experts to make them hopeful again. The way they make them hopeful is mainly by sending them walking up and down the road all day long, and getting in the way of the traffic. Sometimes crude kids yell at them from car windows, "Get outa the way, loonies," and things like that. Once long ago I used to do this. But that is one of the things about me that I hope James and Laura and the others will never know.

I would not do a thing like that now, of course. I know now that the people at Hopeful Hill are not loonies, but just people who need hopeful talking to. And exercise, apparently.

So just because this old lady wanted to go there was no reason for me to be scared of her, any more than I should be scared because she looked like a witch. There are no such things as witches, and there is nobody dangerous at Hopeful Hill, either. Or so they *say*.

All the same, if the well were insulted, and furious, it could easily send a witch after me, or an escaped maniac, or both. Couldn't it?

All this was going through my mind when the old lady suddenly dug me in the ribs with her bony finger. I jumped.

But "Cat got your tongue, boy?" was all she said.

Of course I could perfectly well have given her directions for Hopeful Hill and gone in and shut the door. That is what I started to do.

But then I remembered that the magic is supposed to be made up of doing good turns, and that this was supposed to be my adventure and the others were counting on me.

I knew they hadn't wanted me along in the first

place that day. I knew Lydia didn't have to go to the dentist. And that was really why I'd made the wish on the well, because I was feeling left out. And when Laura was so nice about that, and forgave me, I couldn't let her down now. If the magic had gone wrong, I'd just have to bear whatever brunt there was.

So I said, "I'll come with you and show you."

"Don't let me disturb your party of pleasure," said the old lady. I guess she could see the others peeking from the parlor window.

But I said, "I was just leaving. It's right on my way home. Just a second till I get us a light." And I reached for the pocket flashlight I always carry, for it was really twilight now.

"Lead on, Diogenes," said the old lady. I do not know why she called me that. "I can see in the dark, myself," she added. Somehow this did not make me feel any better about her.

But I just said, "Take my arm, ma'am," and she took it with her skinny claw. If I were good with words, like James, I would probably say that her icy grasp seared my flesh. But it didn't. It just felt like a skinny claw.

As we started down the slope, I looked back and

saw the others in a huddle in the doorway, looking out after us. And when we'd gone a little farther, I could hear them coming along stealthily behind. That made me feel better. So long as they were there, nothing could go very wrong. If anything happened, they'd know what to do about it. They always do. That's what's so wonderful about them.

I would not want them to read some of the things I have written about them in this chapter so far. I admire them so much, things keep slipping out.

I would not want them to read some of the things I have said about myself, either. I'll have to come back and take those parts out, later, but I can't stop now. It's going to be hard enough to tell this story, and worry about sentence errors and errors of taste and getting all the way to the end, without stopping to make changes. Stories are not a thing I am good at. Miss Wilson says I just don't have the gift. She says I should learn to stick to the point. I'll try to do that from now on.

It turned out the old lady didn't need my arm going down the hill at all. She was spry. Most of the time she was hustling me along. Except that she kept stopping, and I guess she *could* see in the dark, because what she stopped for was to pull up more plants and pieces of vine.

Every time she did this she would talk to herself. What she said didn't sound like English, and at first I thought she was speaking mumbo-jumbo spells and gathering evil herbs for her witch's brew. Either that, or she was really crazy and was muttering insane gibberish. But when I stopped being scared long enough to listen, I decided she was just saying the names of plants.

This was interesting. Because you can't grow up in the country without knowing a lot of plants, but you don't always know their names. We got into conversation about this and she pointed out the different ones. Prince's pine I knew, but I didn't know pokeweed or pipsissewa. But this old lady knew just about every plant in that woods.

By the time we got down the hill to the road I was pretty sure she wasn't a witch. Just a poor slightly touched old lady, probably, who had wandered astray. But it did seem too bad that such an active, cheerful old lady should be touched, even slightly.

So I said, "Would you like to talk about your problem?" Just wanting to be friendly, and make small talk.

"My problem?" She sounded surprised.

"Yes. What it is that you're hopeless about. Or have they got you feeling hopeful again by now?"

She began to laugh. But not in a bloodcurdling way at all. And then she told me that she wasn't at Hopeful Hill as a patient. She was one of the doctors, a psychologist she called it. (I had to stop writing this story and go ask James how to spell that word.)

Her job was being a psychologist, but her hobby was nature; so one of the things she did to make people hopeful again was teach them all about plants. And about birds, too.

And then we really began to get along. Because birds have always interested me a lot, for some reason. Only I don't have much chance to talk about them, because most kids seem to think caring about birds is queer. At that last boarding school I went to, that I hated, they called me Birdland, and broke all my Audubon Society records. After that I learned to keep birds to myself. I have never once mentioned them to James and Kip and the others, for fear of what they might think.

But this old lady did not seem to think being interested in birds was queer at all. She hadn't seen a winter wren yet that fall, but I had. And she couldn't imitate the black-throated green warbler worth a darn. I can. But she showed me where there was a pileated woodpecker's nest, just a few yards off my own road.

By the time we came to the private drive that leads to Hopeful Hill, I was really sorry to be saying good-bye. And I almost think maybe she was, too, because she kept her hand on my arm.

"I wonder," she said. "You were asking about my problem. It happens that I do have one. Her name is Sylvia. It occurs to me that you might be able to help me with her."

And she went on to tell me about a little girl patient of hers who was a tragic case.

"You see," she said, "Sylvia lost both her parents, suddenly, in an accident. And it was a terrible shock."

"I know," I said. Because something like that happened to me once, a long time ago.

"The thing is," said the old lady, "Sylvia is sort of frozen in her mind. She won't talk to me or anybody."

"Doesn't she have *any* family left?" I said. Because I only lost a father.

"She has an aunt." The old lady looked cross and witchlike again. "If you can call her that. But *she's* no help." And she went on to say that this aunt had a career, and no time to spend on Sylvia, just money. That was why she had sent her to Hopeful Hill.

"But she doesn't seem to be getting any hope-fuller?" I said.

"No," said the old lady, "she doesn't. That is my problem. I have been wondering if perhaps she wouldn't talk to another child."

It took me a second to realize what she meant. "Me?" I said then, surprised.

"Why not?"

"I'm no great shakes at talking. I've got some friends who could do lots better. Wouldn't you rather ask one of them?"

I had almost forgotten about James and Laura and the others. But now I could hear them coming closer behind us, rustling and whispering, and that was what reminded me. And I think the old lady heard them, too, because her voice went gruff and snappy.

"If I had wanted one of your clever friends," she said, "I would have said so. I'm asking you."

And then I knew this was what the magic had been leading up to, all along, and that my big chance for a good turn was coming, and it was up to me not to fail.

"All right," I said. "I'll try."

I felt solemn as we went up the drive and I looked at Hopeful Hill's big main building, and remembered all the troubled people inside, behind all those curtained windows. And I guess the old lady could tell I was feeling nervous, because she patted my arm.

"Cheer up, Diogenes," she said. "By the way, isn't it time we introduced ourselves?" So I told her my name. When she heard it, she grinned her crocodile grin. "Very well, Gordon T. Witherspoon III," she said. "Will you walk into my parlor?"

And we went inside.

✛ ✛ ✛

This is Laura writing now. Gordy said I should do this bit, because the first adventure ought to have been mine by rights. But I am glad he got it.

When we saw Gordy go off down the hill with that old witch, I could have died. I was sure the magic had gone wrong, and something awful was going to happen to him, and just when I had been so mean to him, too.

But we had promised to be in the adventure; so the

only thing to do was follow. We could see Gordy's flashlight ahead and we kept it in sight, lurking and hanging back so the old witch wouldn't see us.

When we got to the bottom of the hill, it was spooky going along the road in the dark, though we've walked that same road at night hundreds of times and never turned a hair. Once I thought I heard Gordy calling for help, but when we stopped and held our breaths and listened, it didn't seem as if that were it.

"I think he's making birdcalls," James said.

"He couldn't be," I said. But that was exactly what it sounded like.

"She's bewitched him. He thinks he's a twitch-nosed wheedler," said Kip. But I think it was nerves that made him and Lydia giggle.

After that we didn't hear anything more; so we went on.

But when we saw where they were turning in, it didn't seem as if the magic could ever be going to come right again. Because we have always been a little scared of Hopeful Hill. If Deborah weren't so fond of Gordy, I don't think we'd ever have got her up the driveway to where the fateful asylum ominously loomed. We got there just in time to see the dread doors close behind Gordy and the witchlike old lady, with a sound that was awfully final, somehow. We turned to look at each other.

"I swear I'll never pick on Gordy again," I said.

"That's if we ever see him again," Lydia said.

Kip was reconnoitering. "Look!" he said, and we all looked where he pointed.

Behind an uncurtained window on the ground floor a light had gone on, and now we saw Gordy and the old witch come into a room. Another black, witchlike figure came in after them. They talked together for a minute and then the door of the room opened, and we saw the prettiest golden-haired little girl I had ever seen in my life. There was something strange about the way she came into the room, almost as if she were walking in her sleep.

"It's Sleeping Beauty!" Kip said. "The two old witches have brought Gordy to kiss her and wake her up!"

"Some Prince Charming!" said Lydia.

I knew they were only laughing to keep their courage up, but Deborah sputtered indignantly. "I don't know what you mean! I think Gordy'd make a *wonderful* prince!"

37

"I think he's been acting like one," said James. And we all agreed in our hearts. After that we just watched. And the rest of the story is Gordy's.

✝ ✝ ✝

This is Gordy again.

When I followed the old lady into the hall of Hopeful Hill, I didn't know what I'd see. But it wasn't scary a bit, just a big hall with potted plants around and tables, like some dumb old lobby of a hotel.

The old lady led the way into a room at one side,

and another lady followed us in. This second lady had on a black velvet dress, and pearls and a permanent wave, but her face was all frowns and worry lines, and I didn't like her much. I could tell right away she must be the aunt. She didn't look as if she had time for anything. Her eyes moved over all the trailing pieces of vines and plants, and over me, and she sniffed.

"What is all *this,* Doctor Lovely?" she said. That is my old lady's name, Doctor Emma Lovely. At first it seems like a funny name for her, when you think of the way she looks, but the more you know her, it doesn't seem funny at all.

"Just an experiment," was all she said now.

The aunt sniffed again, and I could tell what she thought of the trailing plants, and of me, too. But before she could say anything the door opened, and a nurse in uniform let in a blond-haired little girl and then went away again.

I don't know how to tell you about Sylvia, except that she is pale and thin, and looks a little as if she might break. She is small but bigger than Deborah. In school I guess she would be about in three-one-A. And she is so pretty that all I could do was stand and stare. I did remember to close my mouth, though.

"Gordon, this is Sylvia," Doctor Lovely said. "Sylvia, this is Gordon T. Witherspoon III." And then she took the aunt off to the other end of the room and left me and Sylvia alone.

"Hello," I said.

Sylvia didn't say anything. But she looked at me for a long time and then she smiled.

After that I would have done anything for her, but what could I do? I stood there and wondered, and then I remembered a joke I know. It is a dumb corny joke, I realize, because James and Kip and the others have told me. But I like it, and Deborah always does.

I took my scalp with both hands and pushed it way back so my eyebrows were pulled straight up. And I said, "Mother, haven't you tied my ponytail a little tight?"

Sylvia looked at me for a long time again, as if she didn't know what I meant. And then she laughed.

The aunt jumped as if she'd been shot. "Really, Doctor Lovely," she said. "It is dangerous for Sylvia to be overexcited!"

"Hush," said Doctor Lovely, rather rudely I thought. She was staring at Sylvia as if she expected something to happen.

And then something did. Sylvia said, "What's the third for?"

I didn't understand at first. "What?" I said.

"She said your name was Gordon something the third. What's the third for?"

I found out afterward that those were the first words she had spoken in seven weeks.

So then I told her how I was named for my father and grandfather. And I told her my father was dead, just like hers. Maybe I shouldn't have, but I thought it might be good for her to know that things like that had happened to other people, too. I told her how I lived just across the road and down a way, and about James and Laura and Kip and Lydia and what fun I had with them, now that we were friends. And about Deborah and how she tamed a wicked ogre once.

Sylvia didn't say much, but the questions she asked were smart, and you could tell that she might be troubled in her mind, but she wasn't stupid.

All the while we were talking, the aunt kept sniffing and looking at her watch, and whispering to Doctor Lovely. And finally Doctor Lovely came over to us and said, "I think that is enough conversation for one day. Say good-bye to Gordon, Sylvia."

But Sylvia didn't say good-bye. She reached out and took my hand and said, "Don't go."

I got that feeling where you want to swallow but there's nothing to swallow and you can't. "I guess I have to," I told her. "Maybe I can come back, though. Could I?" And I looked at Doctor Lovely to see if that was all right.

She nodded. "Certainly, Aesculapius." I don't know what she meant by that. I have looked Aesculapius up and he was a famous doctor, which is something I could never be. Though I would like to.

I turned back to Sylvia. "Don't take any wooden nickels," I said. It was dumb, but the best I could do.

The aunt sniffed. But Sylvia laughed again. "Come back tomorrow," she said, and I promised I would.

Doctor Lovely walked with me to the door. "Gordon T. Witherspoon III," she said, "I thank you. I think our experiment was quite a success."

"Couldn't Sylvia be with other kids all the time?" I wondered. "It's wonderful what that can do for you." I knew from experience. "Couldn't she be adopted, and maybe go to school?" I didn't want to say anything against the aunt, or against Hopeful Hill either, but I knew neither one of them could help *me* much, if I were Sylvia.

"Not till she is happier," said Doctor Lovely. "I know this is not the most cheerful place for her," she went on, as if she had read my mind, "but it seems to be the only place, till she is better. I would take her myself, but I am too old and my house is too lonely. And no one will adopt a disturbed child."

She opened the front door and came out on the steps with me. "And now," she said, grinning her crocodile grin, "good night, sweet prince. I must go pacify the aunt, and I believe"—she sort of sniffed the air—"that your friends are waiting."

There isn't much she misses. All the kids were perfectly hidden behind different bushes, and nobody was whispering at all, hardly. But as soon as she was gone, they jumped out and crowded around me, all talking at once.

"Did you hear? *She* called him a prince!" Deborah was saying, jumping up and down the way she does when she's excited.

And "It *is* like Sleeping Beauty. Gordy broke the spell," she said five minutes later, when they'd heard the whole story.

By that time we were going along Silvermine Road, heading for my house because it was nearer. They don't come to my house as often as I go to theirs, on account of Mom. But I remembered that Mom was at a committee meeting that would last through dinner. And we had a lot to talk about, now that the magic had begun again. So I asked them all to supper. I knew it would be all right with Mrs. Sillence our housekeeper, and it was.

"Sure," she said, "it'll be good to have a little life around this morgue." Mrs. Sillence is outspoken. Our house is not a morgue really, only quiet.

We didn't eat at the big table in our dining room that Lydia says is a blow to felicity. Mrs. Sillence served us a buffet supper in the room in front that is called the playroom, only nobody plays anything there. Mom uses it for garden club meetings so the ladies won't track mud on her good rugs.

Mrs. Sillence made her spoon bread, and there was plenty of butter and syrup. Laura was in charge of the meeting, because it is her well, in a way.

"The thing is," she began, "this time the magic took us by surprise. From now on we've got to organize it, and tame it, and decide what we want to do."

But we didn't get organized very far, because everybody had a different idea of what Laura should decide, and told her so. In the middle of all the arguing I heard a noise, a sort of tap-tap-tapping.

I looked. There was a face at the window. At first I couldn't believe it.

"Sylvia!" I said.

Everybody else looked then, and there she was, her nose flattened against the pane and her golden hair falling down on either side of her thin face. And then we all ran for the door and I guess we must have scared her, because when we came out on the lawn, she started to run away. I found myself giving orders. I'd never done a thing like that before. I wouldn't have dared. But I was doing it now.

"Everybody stand back," I said. "I'll handle this." And they let me.

I ran over to where she was, and when she saw it was only me, she stood still and waited. "How did you get here?" I said. "Aren't you cold in that thin dress, without any coat? Don't you want to come inside?"

She looked at me for a minute and then she said, "Yes."

We went in and the others followed. But they hung back and were gentle and I called them over and introduced them one by one. The only piece of spoon bread left was too cold to melt the butter, but I put extra syrup on and Sylvia seemed to like it.

We never did find out exactly how she had got away from Hopeful Hill, but it showed she was smart, all right. She had remembered that I said I lived on the other side of the road a little way along; so she walked till she saw our name on the mailbox.

"I wanted to play with you," she said. And she turned to Deborah sort of shyly. "Tell about the wicked ogre."

Soon they were prattling away in blissful ignorance, as Lydia put it. But when I tried to get up from the table, Sylvia held on to my hand and wouldn't let go. So the others clustered around me and we talked in low voices about what we were going to do with her.

"Couldn't we keep her?" Lydia asked.

"She's not a toy for us to play with," James told her. "We'd have to make arrangements."

I told about Doctor Lovely's thinking Sylvia needed other children.

"That's right," said Laura. "We can't send her back to that gloomy place with those witches, even if one of them *is* a good witch. *We* might adopt her, but we don't have a spare room."

"We do, but we need it for when Dad brings out men from the office," said Kip.

Everybody looked at me. Because everybody knows Lydia's house is sort of run-down and her grandmother is too busy painting pictures to pay attention to anything or anybody, even Lydia.

But *our* house isn't run-down at all and we have lots of spare rooms. And I have always wanted a little brother or sister, though I know if I had one, it couldn't be as pretty as Sylvia. It would be wonderful having Sylvia there with us, and yet the more I thought about Mom I wasn't sure it would be. For Sylvia, I mean.

It is hard to explain about Mom without seeming to be disloyal. She is a wonderful person, but she takes getting used to. And she is busy all the time with committees and the responsibilities of being a social leader, which is what she likes being. I do not know why.

I was afraid that as far as Sylvia was concerned, living with Mom would be just another case of the aunt. Much as I hated to give her up, I thought the only thing to do was telephone Doctor Emma Lovely.

Sylvia still wouldn't let go my hand; so James did the telephoning. Three minutes later Doctor Lovely came whizzing around our driveway on two wheels, in her little old rattlebang car.

Sylvia seemed glad to see her, and smiled and said, "Hello." But when she learned the doctor was going to take her back to Hopeful Hill, her face puckered as if she were going to cry.

Doctor Lovely looked at me, sort of helplessly, and I knelt down by Sylvia, feeling awful and hoping the magic would help me say the right thing.

"Sylvia," I said, "I'm awfully glad you came to call. Come again, anytime. Tomorrow I'll come calling on *you,* the way I said. I'll come every day. Maybe I could bring the kids with me."

I looked at Doctor Lovely to see if that would be all right and she nodded. "Only not all at once."

Sylvia's face unpuckered a little. She pointed at Deborah. "Her first." And then we all went out to the driveway.

Just as Doctor Lovely and Sylvia were starting up, we saw Mom's limousine turn in, with Craddock our chauffeur at the wheel. And right away everybody else said good-bye quick, and jumped in Doctor Lovely's car, too. That is how Mom affects people sometimes. That is how I had been afraid she would affect Sylvia.

I hated to see them go. But Sylvia leaned out of the car and blew me a kiss good-bye.

"Really, Gordy," said Mom a few seconds later, coming into the playroom and looking at the remains of the spoon bread. "What has been going on? And who were all those people in the drive?"

"Oh, nothing," I told her, sort of airily. "I merely had a few friends in for supper."

And I went upstairs feeling good about the way I'd handled things. But of course after I got in bed I realized I hadn't solved anything. Sylvia would never get really well at Hopeful Hill. I knew that, and I thought Doctor Lovely did, too. It didn't seem to me the magic had things under control at all. I lay awake puzzling about it for a long time, and when I went to sleep, I dreamed about it all night. In the morning I had to be called three times.

Maybe that is why I was extra dumb in school the next day. Not that I am ever extra bright. And not that you have to be very bright in my class.

When I got Mom to send me to public school, I thought I'd be in the same room with James and Kip and Laura and Lydia, and everything would be wonderful. But I might have known.

I am not really like them at all. I haven't read lots of interesting books and I can't think quickly, and it is only right that they should be in the bright class and I should end up in the dumb one.

The school can call it six-one-B if it wants to, but it is the dumb class and everybody knows it. That's why we have to have a really tough teacher like Miss Wilson who can handle us. Miss Wilson has been teaching since about the year one, and there is not much that she does not know about handling dumb kids. I am not the dumbest kid in the class. I am just somewhere down near the bottom.

But this morning I seemed to be dumber than anybody. We were having improper fractions, and I couldn't seem to understand how to make them proper again. I kept thinking about Sylvia instead. Finally Miss Wilson said I'd just have to stay after school and she'd go over it all with me then, and not waste the time of the entire class.

My heart sank, because I had promised to call on Sylvia at Hopeful Hill, and if Miss Wilson kept me, I might be too late.

But the whole day went on just like that. I was as bad in history and English as I was in arithmetic.

By the time it was three o'clock and I was staying after, I was so sleepy and worried and mixed up that I couldn't even remember what a least common denominator was. Miss Wilson put her book down. "Gordon Witherspoon," she said, "exactly *what* is on your mind?"

I decided to throw myself on her mercy. Maybe the magic would melt her. Because nothing else would.

So I said, "Miss Wilson, do you believe in wishes?" And I went on to tell her about the well, and about everything that had happened.

I guess the magic worked, for by the time I finished about Sylvia, Miss Wilson didn't look like herself at all. Usually she is sort of hard and dry, and as if she'd been breathing too much chalk dust. Now her face was soft.

"The poor little thing," she murmured. "The poor little thing." Then she pulled herself together and shut her book with a snap. "Gordon Witherspoon," she said, "this foolishness can wait. Come with me."

We got our hats and coats from the cloakroom and I followed her down the stairs and into her car, which was a treat, because she drives a Thunderbird, and *fast*. First we stopped at her house, which is big and white on a big neat lawn on Main Street, and Miss Wilson ran inside. She was out again in ten seconds, carrying a big box tied with pink ribbon. And we headed for Hopeful Hill.

In the lobby we had a little trouble with a bossy nurse, because it wasn't visiting hours. But Miss Wilson was grand. "I," she said, "am Ermentrude Wilson." Just as if she were saying she was Queen Elizabeth. So now I know what Miss Wilson's first name is. On our grade cards she always puts just "E. Wilson," and no wonder. But I will never tell.

Just then Doctor Lovely appeared, and after that it was all right. We went into the little side room and pretty soon a nurse brought Sylvia, just like the day before. Sylvia ran right over to me and took my hand.

"Hello," she said. "You're late." And she smiled. When she saw the smile, Miss Wilson went all soft and started murmuring, "Poor little thing" again.

Sylvia's face began to pucker and I was worried. It seemed to me she had probably been called a poor little thing often enough already, and it is no good feeling sorry for yourself. I know.

But Miss Wilson has sense, and right away she brisked up again. She looked at me and maybe I gave her an idea. Because suddenly she did that same joke I'd told her about, pushing back her scalp and saying her ponytail was too tight. On Miss Wilson it looked *awful*. Sylvia laughed and laughed.

And then Miss Wilson said, "Sylvia, I have brought you a present," and handed her the box, but sensibly let her untie the pink ribbon herself.

I would be the last to know about dolls, but I would say the doll in that box was tops, for a doll. Sylvia's eyes got big and round and she said, "Oh!"

"It was mine when I was your age," Miss Wilson told her. "No one has played with it since. At my house I have every doll and dollhouse I have ever owned. I was saving them for . . . but never mind. Perhaps you would like to come and see them."

And then she left Sylvia playing with the doll and drew Doctor Lovely aside. They seemed to forget I was there. But I could still hear.

"I wonder," she said, "if you would let me take Sylvia. I have a large home and ample means. I have been teaching school in this town for twenty-five years. The Board of Education will vouch for me. Perhaps just at first she could visit in my classroom, till she is ready to join the third grade. And after school"—she smiled rather sadly I thought—"I have all the time in the world. I have always wanted a child of my own."

Doctor Lovely looked at her, and I guess she approved of what she saw. "Why not ask Sylvia?" she said.

"Sylvia," said Miss Wilson, "would you like to come visit me and my dollhouses for a while? Perhaps you might even want to stay."

Sylvia turned to me. "Would you come and see me?"

"Sure," I said. "But you'll be making friends of your own once you're in the third grade." I do not know any of the kids in three-one-A personally, but I am sure there are lots of good types.

Sylvia smiled round at all of us. "All right," she said.

It seemed to me the adventure was over. I had to hand it to the magic for working everything out just fine. I started edging away, but Miss Wilson looked up. "Wait," she said, and she followed me to the door.

"Gordon," she went on, "I know that you have friends in Mrs. Van Nest's class. I have been wondering if you wouldn't be happier with them. It is a fast group, of course, but I think if you enjoyed school more, you might do better work and be able to keep up."

I couldn't believe it. The thought of being with

Kip and James and Laura and Lydia was too much. Still, maybe they'd get tired of me if I were there all the time. And they would be disgusted if they saw how dumb I can be in class, sometimes.

But that wasn't really it. The thing was, it seemed mean to leave Miss Wilson now, just when I was getting to know what she was really like. Perhaps I could help her with Sylvia, too, at first.

So I said, "Let's wait till midyears, and then see."

Miss Wilson's face looked funny. "Thank you, Gordon," she said. And then she went down on her knees by Sylvia again.

I looked at Doctor Lovely. She grinned. "Congratulations, Hippocrates," she said.

I do not know why she keeps calling me these names. But I grinned a crocodile grin right back. "So long," I said. "I'll be seeing you." And I ran out of Hopeful Hill and all the way down Silvermine Road as fast as I could, to tell the others all about it.

3

Laura Organizes

This is Laura writing now because it was my turn next.

If this were a real book, I would probably start out by telling how we waited for Gordy after school that day, and how he didn't come, and how worried we all were. And I would say things like "Meanwhile, back at the school" and "had I but known."

But what would be the point, when you already know exactly where Gordy was and what he was doing?

It is those parts in books that James and I always skip. I only mention it at all because it was while we were waiting for Gordy that Dicky LeBaron came swaggering up to us, and you might as well know about him now as later. He was wearing black denim trousers and motorcycle boots and a black leather jacket as usual, and he was just as hateful-acting as usual, too.

"If you're looking for your rich friend," he said, "he had to stay after." And then he sort of sneered, and went swaggering away.

Lydia started after him, but I stopped her. There is no point in talking to some people. Consider the source is what I say.

Dicky LeBaron is the kind of person that I used to think only happened in cities, and then people write plays and articles about them and call them juvenile delinquents. It was quite a shock to find that they can turn up in the country, too.

Dicky had never been anything but insulting to me, and I was sure he bullied Gordy in six-one-B, though Gordy would never say. As for Lydia, she and Dicky were old enemies. Lydia often boasted of what she would do to Dicky LeBaron if she had the chance, and sometimes I thought it might be interesting to let her try. But right now our bus was waiting.

In the bus we forgot Dicky LeBaron and argued about what to do next with the magic. James thought Gordy's staying after school meant we were free to take over and rescue Sylvia from durance vile. When we passed Hopeful Hill, he and Kip wanted to get out and deploy about the building, at least. But I thought we ought to go to the red house and wait for Gordy. So that's what we did, and pretty soon he came running down the road and told us all about Sylvia and Miss Wilson.

I thought it was a beautiful happy ending like a movie, but Lydia was indignant. "What kind of magic is that?" she said. "Saving her from one old witch just to hand her over to another!"

Gordy looked stubborn. "You don't know Miss Wilson," he said. "She's all right."

Lydia wasn't satisfied. "If *I'd* been there, the ending would have been different. But the whole adventure just skipped everybody but Gordy!"

"Don't you see why? I do," I said. "It's because I was mean and grabby when Gordy made the wish. So the well left us right out of the whole thing."

"Moral lessons," said Lydia. "When I get *my* adventure, I'm not going to let any old moral lesson come into it at all."

That is how she always talks. As to whether or not it worked out that way when she came to have her turn, let that remain to be seen.

I will not tell about the next few days, because James said we would leave out the times when nothing happened. Suffice to say that nothing did.

Except that every day Gordy went to see Sylvia and took a different one of us along each time. So far as anyone could see, Sylvia and Miss Wilson were getting along fine. "But just wait," said Lydia.

All this while, of course, we kept our eyes peeled for good turns that needed doing, wherever we went. But no long-lost heirs or damsels in distress were forthcoming, and by Saturday I decided we should stay home and try letting the magic come to us. There were a lot of leaves that needed raking, and maybe if we attended to those, the magic would see how useful we were being and take a hint.

So Kip and Gordy and Lydia and I raked, while Deborah buried herself in the piles of leaves and James sat on the wellhead and read us interesting bits from the *Advertiser* out loud.

The *Advertiser* is our town newspaper and it comes out every week, but James is the only one of us who ever looks at it much. James likes to keep up with everything. He even reads the letters to the editor. It was one of those that he read to us now.

"Dear Sir:

Here's good luck to our new
railroad station.

A Well-Wisher"

"Honestly, did you ever hear of anything so feeble?" he went on. "If I didn't have anything better than that to say, I wouldn't write a letter to the editor at all."

"What does it mean?" I wondered. "We don't have a new railroad station. Do we?"

"Maybe it's a secret code," said Kip.

"Maybe it's somebody who's got a well like ours, with wishes in it," said Deborah, poking her head up from the nearest leaf pile.

James stared at her. "Out of the mouths of babes!" he said.

"You mean," said Kip, "that maybe there're other people with magic in this town, too?"

"Why not?" said James. "When you think of all the magic there must be, floating around. And when you think of all the wells people have in their front yards. Maybe it's a whole organization, and we've just joined the club."

This was an exciting idea. "Or if there isn't," I said, "we could start one. We could organize all the people with wells, to work together. If we all wished at the same time, there's nothing we couldn't do. I think it's a sign. I think it's what the magic wants. James was sitting right on the well when he read the letter. Probably the magic seeped through. Probably if he'd been sitting somewhere else, there wouldn't have been any letter at all. Anyway, we've got a name now. We're Well-Wishers from today on. We wish everybody well, don't we? It stands to reason."

Since it was my turn for an adventure, everybody had to agree. But I think they all liked the idea, too. We decided to start right out and investigate the wells on our own Silvermine Road first. But we took our bikes along, because there was no telling how far the organization might spread. Gordy rode Deborah on his handlebars as usual.

But first I went over to our own well and looked down. "Thank you for the message," I told it. "Did we get it right? Now just keep on cooperating, please."

And we started up Silvermine Road.

The first well we came to was awfully pretty, with iron curlicues all over it and vines trained around. But when we looked down, we saw that it wasn't a real well at all, but just decoration. Some people would do anything for show.

The next well had a sign on the lawn saying, "Beware of the dog," and we didn't and we wished we had. I don't know how many wells we missed before the dog got tired of chasing us and went home.

The third well ought to have been the lucky one, but while we were investigating it, a little old lady came out of the house and said yes, it was a wishing well, and every morning when the morning glories said good morning to her, a dear little fairy looked out of the well and said good morning, too. This was discouraging, but we were polite about it.

But some of the other wells belonged to quite understanding people who said that they hadn't tried wishing yet, but they certainly would at the first opportunity. I wrote their names down in my notebook, and they promised to let us know what happened. And one of them gave us a whole half of a Lady Baltimore cake. But it seemed that if there was a secret club called the Well-Wishers, we were the only members.

The Lady Baltimore cake was delicious, though. We ate it in the little old forgotten cemetery by the corner of Wilton Road. Kip says picnicking in cemeteries is grisly, but I like this one. It is quiet, and old enough to feel historical. And there is nothing like munching some good cake in a quiet place to make a person think, I find.

Sure enough, just as I was finishing the last crumbs, I had an idea.

"You know what?" I said. "That part of the letter about the railroad station. That could mean something, too."

"Like a clue?" said Kip.

"Why not? Magic doesn't just go round saying things at random. It's all supposed to add up. I think we ought to head for the station right now, and see what happens." So it turned out to be a good thing we'd brought our bikes along. But maybe the magic had attended to that, too.

When we came down Elm Street, a train had just pulled in that Kip said was the one-eighteen. He is good with timetables. There were only two passengers left on the platform, and as we coasted into the station yard, they drove off in a taxi. James and Lydia were sure they were part of the magic, and wanted us to jump in the next taxi and say, "Follow that cab!" and see what adventure the people would lead us to.

But we only had fifty cents among us, and besides, I had seen who the two people were and I knew where they would lead us. It was Florence Squibb and her mother, back from the dentist's in Stamford, and the only place they would lead us would be the Squibbs' house on Whiffletree Lane. And Florence Squibb is a perfectly nice girl, and fine for trading movie stars' pictures with when all else fails, but there is no magic in her.

"No," I said, "I think we're meant to stick to wells. I think we're meant to start from the station and try the first well we see." So we went along Park Street, because it was closest.

But there are no wells on Park Street. It is all neat houses in rows, almost like being in the city. Later on, though, it runs into Old Stamford Road, and there is country again. We went past the Bird Sanctuary, and Gordy revealed hidden depths, telling us what the different birds were and all about them, till we begged him to stop.

It is wonderful what magic can do for people. I have never heard Gordy even mention a robin before. But now it is almost as if *he* were the Sleeping Beauty and Sylvia had broken the spell and wakened *him* up.

But there was no well in the Bird Sanctuary. We didn't count the birdbath.

We were beginning to be discouraged when we heard a voice calling us ahead. That seemed like a hopeful sign, and we urged our flagging bikes forward.

The voice turned out to belong to a little old man at a roadside stand, and now we could hear his words.

"Apples, ripe apples, Winesaps, Northern Spies, Greenings!"

And we saw the apples piled round on shelves, bright red and light green and mixed, and all rounder and juicier-looking than you'd ever find in any store. We saw the orchard, too, stretching out on all sides, the trees thick with fruit. Next to the stand was a sign, "Appledore Orchard, Adam Appledore, Prop." Judging by looks, we felt sure the little old man could only be Adam Appledore himself. His face was the shape of an apple and the color of an apple, too. A red one, that is.

It had been a long pull from the cemetery to the station, and by now the Lady Baltimore cake seemed long ago and far away. So we put our fifty cents together and Mr. Appledore made us up a wonderful basket, of all the kinds he had except the cooking ones.

James bit into a Delicious. "And rightly named," he said.

"Eat your fill," said Mr. Appledore. "It's your last chance."

And then we noticed another sign, to one side. "This property is condemned," it said.

"Poor orchard. What's it done?" said Deborah, when we had explained to her what "condemned" meant.

"Not a thing," said Mr. Appledore, "except earn a living for me and mine these forty year. And for my father before me and his father before him."

"But that's terrible," I said. "A beautiful big orchard like this."

"Ayeh," said Mr. Appledore. "That it is. Beautiful in fall with the fruit of them and beautiful in spring with the bloom of them and beautiful in winter with just the shape of them, them trees are. What with feeding and spraying and picking 'em, them trees has been like friends of mine, from a boy. And it's sad to see one friend pass on at my time o' life, not speakin' o' two thousand and two, that being the sum in question."

"Where are they passing on *to?*" said James. "What's going to happen to them?"

"Lumberyard," said Mr. Appledore, "or firewood. All cut down to make room for this newfangled railway station!"

At that we all looked at each other. And I was sure we were on the right track.

"Couldn't they build their station someplace else?" asked Lydia.

"No place else near the railroad line big enough for the parking lot," said Mr. Appledore. "Pesky overgrown station wagons! Danged commuters!"

"The town's paying you, isn't it?" said Kip in rather a peculiar voice.

"Ayeh," Mr. Appledore admitted. "They're paying me well enough. But where can I find another orchard this size without emigratin' to foreign parts? Nearest one is three miles across town. And I like this here neighborhood right here. There've always been Appledores on Old Stamford Road."

"Mr. Appledore," I said, "do not despair. We'll save you. We were *sent* to save you. I don't know how just yet, but we will."

"That's as may be," said Mr. Appledore.

And then I gave the others a look, and we moved

on, because I thought it would be more delicate to discuss Mr. Appledore's problem in private. There wasn't a doubt in my mind, or James's or Lydia's or Gordy's or Deborah's, about the good turn the magic wanted us to do. We walked slowly, wheeling our bikes, so as to have more breath for talking.

"We've got to save those apples," I said. "Only how?"

"I don't see why we need a new station in the first place," said James, and I agreed. Personally we hadn't been near the station since we first moved here from New York City, until today. Because who would want to go anywhere when we had the country, and magic, too?

"I think there ought to be a town meeting," said Lydia, "like before."

She was thinking of the time when the town wanted to build a new school and some people tried to stop it. But we worked our magic on the town meeting, and today the new school is going up and almost finished.

Kip spoke for the first time in quite a while. He was frowning, which was unusual, because he is mostly a happy-go-lucky type without a serious thought in his head.

"I don't think this is quite the same thing," he said. "I think this time there're two sides to it."

I looked at him, surprised.

"It's all very well for *you*," he went on, to James and me. "Your father's a writer and works at home. And Lydia's grandmother's an artist and Gordy's mother's just rich and doesn't do anything. But *my* Pop's a businessman and his business is in New York. He goes in there every day so we can stay out here. And if he's willing to make that sacrifice, I think at least he ought to have a place to park his car. And the old station lot isn't half big enough; I've heard him say so."

There did seem to be some sense to this. Somebody has to be in New York, I suppose, or they wouldn't have it. "But those wonderful apples!" I said.

"I'm sorry about them," said Kip, "but I think maybe they'll have to go. I think maybe if you try to save them, you'll be like those people who didn't want the new school because it would spoil our lovely old village quality. I think you'll be standing in the way of progress. And you can't. Nobody can."

Kip certainly can be convincing when he tries. Maybe because he doesn't try very often. But I felt like a balloon that somebody's pricked a hole in. "If the magic didn't mean us to save the apples," I said, "what *did* it mean?"

"The thing is," said James, "to find a way for Mr. Appledore to leave his orchard and have it, too."

We were so deep in thought and talk that we weren't looking around or noticing where we were going. But Deborah has sharp eyes and never misses anything.

"There's a well," she said now.

We had forgotten all about wells, but we looked, and there one was, in the middle of a big garden by the side of the road. There was a hedge all round the garden, and a gate at the entrance. The hedge was overgrown and the gate was off its hinges.

The mailbox by the gate said "Smith." Someone had painted a border of bright flowers around the name, but the paint was peeling and the mailbox hung all crooked.

The garden looked lovely at first, but when we came closer, we saw that the lawn was full of dandelions and plantains and there were tent caterpillars on the shrubs. Plants bloomed in the flower beds, but they hadn't been staked and the tall ones had fallen down and were lying all over the low ones.

We stood looking over the gate and now a lady

came from the house. She was a very large lady and not very young or very beautiful, but she moved as if she thought she were both. She had on a lot of trailing scarves and a big garden hat, and as she came swaying down the path, she suddenly threw back her head and screamed. Or at least that's what I thought at first, but then I realized she was probably singing.

And Kip, who is a hi-fi fiend, said later that it was the "Jewel Song" from *Faust,* and grand opera.

"'Ah, what gems with their magic glare deceive my eye? Ah!'" She sang, going up higher than you would think anyone could, or would want to. She leaned over the well. "'Marguerite, is it you? Is it you, or some lovely vision?'" she sang, peering into the well as if she expected to find the truth at the bottom of it.

I led the way through the gate and up the path.

"I beg your pardon, ma'am," I said. "Is that a wishing well?"

The lady did not seem surprised to see six strange children in her garden. But then she is a very vague lady, as we were to learn.

"Who knows?" she said. "I was just wishing there were someone to hear me, and now there you are!

So perhaps it is. Now you can tell your children and your children's children that you were the last to hear the golden notes of Marguerite Salvini!"

"Gosh," said Kip. "Is that who you are? My pop's got an old record of you."

"Records?" said the lady. "What are records? They are as nothing to those who have seen Marguerite Salvini in the flesh!"

And as we surveyed her ample curves, I am sure we were all ready to believe that this was true.

"The mailbox says Smith," said James, ever one for getting the facts straight.

"So it does," said the lady. "That was my secret. When crowned heads bowed before the great Marguerite Salvini, little did they think that she was born plain Maggie Smith. Yet plain Maggie Smith became the toast of Europe. In Paris they drank champagne from my slipper. In Rome they unharnessed my horses and pulled my carriage through the streets!"

"And then," I said, "I suppose you wearied of the vain pomp and show?"

"Yes," said the lady, "that's exactly what I did. What joy, I thought, to be plain Maggie Smith again and live in a cottage by the side of the road and be a friend to man! But it has not worked out at all. The roof leaks and the peas failed and the corn got borers and the beans came up upside down!" And she raised her voice in song. "'Farewell to the bright visions I once fondly cherished. Already the roses that decked me have perished!'"

"There's a rose still," said Deborah, picking a late red one and handing it to her. The lady raised it to her nose and dropped it again. There was a Japanese beetle on it.

"You see?" she said. "And as for the apples . . ."

"Apples?" I said, excited. "You have apples?"

"A whole orchard full." She waved an arm, and for the first time I noticed apple trees covering the hill beyond the house for as far as I could see. "But alas. All wormy."

"If they're wormy, the trees must need spraying," said James.

"Sprrrraying?" said Madame Salvini, getting more trilled r's into it than you'd think one word could hold. "What do I know of spraying? Or digging or weeding or hammering nails? What has an artist to do with these?" And she was off again. "'Love and music, these have I lived for, nor ever have harmed a living being. The poor and distressful by stealth I have succored. . . .'"

"Yes, it's very good of you, I'm sure," I interrupted when she paused for breath, "but why do it by stealth? I know somebody distressful you could be succoring right this minute."

"It would be being a friend to man, too," Kip put in.

"Aha!" said Madame Salvini, rolling her eyes. "If we begin to speak of *men* . . ."

"We don't," I said quickly, because she looked as if she might be going to tell us the story of her life. "What Kip meant was a *hired* man."

"How could I hire him? My little income has dwindled away. And still the place goes from rack to ruin!"

"I think," I said, "I may be able to fix that. Wait right there. We'll be back." And we started up the road. Nobody needed to be told where we were heading. The sound of Madame Salvini's voice followed us, borne upon the breeze.

"'Ah, ye beautiful songbirds, I hear your pinions! What seek ye? Whither going? Who knows?'" she sang. A crow flew over. "Caw," it said.

When we reached Mr. Appledore's stand, he was

busy selling a basket of crab apples to a woman in a Chevy. We waited till he was free and then I stepped forward.

"Mr. Appledore," I said, "all is not lost. I *told* you not to despair. Follow me." And I took hold of his arm.

"What's all this?" said Mr. Appledore, hanging back. "Where you taking me? What about my stand and my cashbox?"

"Oh dear." I turned to James. "I suppose it's up to me to stay and watch them."

But Gordy gave me a little push. "Go on. It's your adventure. I had mine. I don't mind waiting here one bit." Honestly, you would never believe how that boy has changed.

Deborah volunteered to stay and keep him company, and the rest of us hustled Mr. Appledore along. As we drew near the house with the hedge, we could hear Madame Salvini still rendering arias, but Mr. Appledore wasn't scared away, the way I was afraid he would be. He even seemed to like it.

"High voice, ain't she?" he said. "I admire a high voice in a woman. Pity she don't sing something a body could hum. 'Home on the Range' now, or 'Trees.'"

"Speaking of trees," I began, trying to call his attention to the orchard.

But he was looking over the gate at Madame Salvini. He seemed to like what he saw, large or not. I introduced them, and Mr. Appledore swept off his cap.

"Afternoon, ma'am. You farming this place all on your own? Stony ground hereabouts. Hard job for a frail woman." His eye rested on her flowing contours. "Hard job for a woman," he corrected himself.

He went through the gate and walked about, eyeing the place from all angles. He looked down at the lawn. "Dandylions. Fruit knife for those. Get 'em all out. Taproots." He looked at the flower beds. "String needed there. Green kind. Won't show. Or pea-brush. Kerosene for them beetles." He looked at the house, went closer, and dug his penknife into the boards. "Dry rot. New sills wanted."

Madame Salvini sighed. "I am afraid it is all Greek to me. All I hoped for was peace, and a quiet nest to rest in, now my song is over."

"Not much peace about a farm," said Mr. Appledore. "Not much rest, neither. One year's seeding, ten years' weeding. Once a place starts going downhill, there's no stopping it."

Then at last his gaze fell on the apple trees and he was silent. He was silent so long I began to be worried.

"Shocking state, them trees," he said finally.

"Are they that bad?" I said. "Past repair? Not worth bothering with?"

"Wouldn't say that," he muttered. "Wouldn't say that ezzactly. Takes a lot o' killing, a apple tree does. Nitrogen. Lime sulfur. Arsenic of lead. Wouldn't

happen overnight, mind you. Rome wasn't built in a day. But lemme at them trees, and I'd have 'em bearing again good as new. And no worms."

I felt good. "You'd enjoy it, too, wouldn't you?"

"Nothin' perks up a farmer's heart like reclaimin' lost land," he admitted.

"And the town will be paying you a lot of money, for *your* orchard," Kip reminded him.

"And you could afford to pay Madame Salvini a good rent for hers," said James.

"And then *she* could afford to fix her place up," said Lydia.

"And you could give her pointers," I said. "You see? It all adds up. And there would still be Appledores on Old Stamford Road."

Mr. Appledore was silent again. His gaze rested on Madame Salvini. Then he spoke. "Ayeh. It might not be so bad."

"Not bad? It'd be perfect," I said. "You'd be a sort of team."

Madame Salvini sighed. "I was a team with Martinelli once. People came from all over the world to hear us."

"And this way they'll probably come from all over

the world to taste your apples," I said. "And that ought to be just as good, in a way."

Madame Salvini sighed. "It is tempting," she said. "But no. It is not to be. I should never have deserted my public. Dozens write to me every day, asking when I will come back and shower my golden notes upon them again. And that's what I must do. It is my duty to share my great gift."

"Are you sure?" I said, for her notes had not sounded as golden as that to me. "Wouldn't it be better to quit while the quitting's good?"

"At least let me see inside the house before I go," said Mr. Appledore. "Hain't been in that house in thirty year. Old Mis' Jenkins lived in it then. She couldn't farm, neither."

Madame Salvini sighed. "Very well," she said. "It's nothing to me. 'Home no more home to me, whither shall I wander?'"

She drifted toward the house, and Mr. Appledore followed her and held the door for her and went in after her, and that seemed to be that.

In a way, I supposed, it had worked out fine. If Madame Salvini were leaving, Mr. Appledore could probably buy her orchard cheap. But somehow I felt disappointed. It all seemed to be just business, and with no romance in it. I had hoped for more from the magic than that. And yet the more I went on thinking about it, I couldn't imagine Mr. Appledore drinking champagne out of anyone's slipper, and neither could the others.

"Well," I said, "I suppose we might as well go home."

"We can't," said James. "Remember the apple stand?"

I had forgotten, but now I remembered. We went back up Old Stamford Road, and there Gordy and Deborah were, waiting patiently. They had taken in eighty-seven cents.

And then we all waited, but not so patiently, and the minutes kept going slower and no cars stopped, and it began to be dark and time for supper, and we were all hungry, but there was nothing to eat but apples.

We had no money, but we put in an IOU each time. But apples do not go a long way when you are starving.

"I for one," said Lydia when she had downed her third, "will never save an orchard again. I think they ought to be stamped out."

Gordy uttered a burp. At any other time we would have lectured him on manners, but right now we felt a sympathetic bond. We would have all done the same thing if we could.

And it was then, as spirits ebbed and the flesh was weakest, that Dicky LeBaron came round the corner, riding in a stripped-down jalopy with a couple of tough older boys. He goes around with the worst kids in the high school and toadies up to them something awful.

When they saw us, they stopped their car with a squeal of brakes and just sat there looking at us with nasty grins on all three of their faces, and my heart sank even further. But it seemed to be Gordy they wanted to bully most.

"Well, if it isn't Gordon T. Witherspoon III!" said the one driving.

"What you doing in this low-down common neighborhood, rich boy?" said the other high school boy.

Dicky LeBaron was less insulting, but he was insulting enough. "Hey, Gordy," he said in lordly tones, "toss me an apple."

Gordy's face looked whiter than usual. But he

was spunky, as always. "No," he said. "They're not mine."

The two high school boys pretended they couldn't believe their ears. "Did I hear Gordon T. Witherspoon III say *no* to you, Dicky boy?" said the first one.

"Do you let rich little squirts talk rough to you like that, Dicky boy?" said the second. "I thought you were the boss of six-one-B!"

Dicky LeBaron's face got red. "Come on, hand it over," he said gruffly.

James stepped up by Gordy. "We're minding this stand for a friend," he said. "If you want to buy an apple, they're five cents each."

The boy who was driving flicked his eyes over James. "Boy Scouts," he said. And he spat into the road.

"Do-gooders," agreed the second boy. "Teacher's pets."

Dicky LeBaron shifted in the car seat as if he were uncomfortable. "Aw, come on," he said. "Let's get outa here."

"Wait," said the second boy. "Got to teach these teacher's pets a lesson first. Whaddaya say we wreck their stand for them?"

Dicky LeBaron opened his mouth, but before he

could say anything, the boy who was driving suddenly headed his car straight at us and stepped on the gas, and we all had to scatter and jump.

Of course he swerved at the last minute and went peeling on up the road, but one wheel did graze a corner of the stand and apples started toppling off and rolling every which way.

Lydia didn't waste time on words. She just reached down and grabbed up one of the apples and sent it after the car. She can throw straight as any boy.

The apple hit the driver on the back of the neck, and it must have hurt, because he let out a yell and jammed on his brakes and started climbing out of the car. But just then some grown-ups appeared, walking along the road, and he must have thought better of it. Because he got back behind the wheel and drove away.

"Darn," said Lydia. "I wanted to hit that Dicky LeBaron. Wait till it's my turn for an adventure. I'll show him."

"He wasn't as bad as the others," I pointed out. "And the magic's not for getting even; it's for doing good turns."

"To squelch Dicky LeBaron," said Lydia, "would be a good turn to the whole human race."

And then we helped Deborah and the boys pick up apples.

We were still at it when the grown-ups we'd noticed before came nearer. But when I looked up and really saw them, I couldn't believe my eyes.

It was Madame Salvini and Mr. Appledore, but what a change! They were walking hand in hand, and she was rolling her eyes at him and hanging on his every word, and when we talked to them, she hardly seemed to notice us at all. It just showed I shouldn't have been in such a hurry to criticize the magic. It knows what it's doing.

Or maybe Mr. Appledore has hidden depths, like Gordy.

"I'm afraid some apples got spilled," James said.

"Oh, that," said Madame Salvini vaguely, not taking her eyes from Mr. Appledore.

"We ate some, too," said Kip, "but we kept a record of every one."

"Oh, them," said Mr. Appledore. "Take them and welcome. I got me a new orchard now. Down to Maggie's place. We're pardners from now on. They can build their pesky station and plow my land under anytime they choose. Eat your fill."

James shuddered. "Thanks. We already did." But I was excited.

"Is it really all settled? What about your public?"

Madame Salvini rolled her eyes at Mr. Appledore. "Adam has convinced me. The simple life is best. We will be a . . . how do you say it? A team. It will be paradise regained and we will be Adam and Eve!"

"Good," I said. "I guess that proves your well *is* a wishing well, all right. And you can be our first real new members."

I wrote their names down in my notebook and told them all about the Well-Wishers' Club, but I don't think they listened much. They kept looking at each other. When we left, they were strolling back toward Madame Salvini's house, still hand in hand. And I guess Mr. Appledore was teaching Madame Salvini a new song, because her voice followed us as we biked along.

"Listen," I said. And we all heard the words she was singing.

"'I think that I shall never see a poem lovely as a trrrrree!'"

"There," I said. And everybody agreed.

When James and Deborah and I got home, we were late for supper and it was baked apples for dessert, but I didn't mind. The Well-Wishers were organized, and from now on we would find new members all the time, and when a big important wish came along, there would be lots of us to wish together, and there was nothing we wouldn't be able to do! Or at least that's the way I planned it.

That's the way it worked out, too, more or less.

But of course first Lydia had to try using the magic for her own fell purpose.

She can't say I didn't warn her about moral lessons and turning the other cheek and the meek inheriting the earth and biters getting bit and vengeance being an idle dream. But there are some things a person has to learn for himself. Or herself, as the case may be.

I do not think Lydia is ready to inherit the earth yet. But she did learn a lot when her time came. The well certainly made her learn it the hard way, though. But I must not be grabby about the magic again. Let each one tell his part.

It is Lydia's turn now.

4

Lydia Learns

This is Lydia writing this chapter.

Ever since I can remember, I have always hated Dicky LeBaron. Before I met Laura and James and learned how to make friends, he was my worst deadly enemy.

I knew him pretty well in those days, because we were in the same room in school for ages, and both had to stay after a lot, but not for the same reasons. *I* got into trouble by stupid showing off, but Dicky LeBaron was the kind whose idea of fun is breaking things.

The year we were in the fifth grade he and his awful older-boy friends went around all winter knocking people's mailboxes down. They seemed to do it to *our* box oftener than to anybody else's, maybe because Dicky didn't like me any better than I liked him.

One cold night I lay in wait for him behind a tree,

and when he and his friends came up to the mailbox, I threw a pail of water over them and escaped on a horse I used to have. After that it was war.

But the next summer Laura and James moved to town and I began to know them and Kip and Gordy, and everything changed. And that fall Dicky got put in six-one-B and I mostly forgot him.

Not that Dicky is dumb. He comes from a poor background, but he is smart. But I guess Mr. Colfax, the principal, thought Miss Wilson could handle him better. Mrs. Van Nest is a wonderful teacher, but soft. She believes in letting the young idea shoot.

But if Dicky LeBaron heard a teacher say a thing like that, he would probably show up in class next day with a BB gun.

The talk around school was that Dicky picked on Gordy a lot, in six-one-B. Sometimes James got wind of things that had happened, and wanted to give Dicky a dose of his own medicine, but Gordy would never let him. I could understand why. A boy has to stand on his own two feet. Even if they are both left feet, the way Gordy's sometimes seem to be.

But aside from that, up to the day of the apples I had begun to think of Dicky LeBaron as a thing of the past.

And even afterwards I might have listened to Laura's advice and not tried to get even, if Dicky had let us alone. But he didn't, from that day on.

The very next afternoon we were having a meeting in the secret house when I heard a scrabbling noise outside. I went out on the stoop to investigate, and there was Dicky, climbing up and trying to peek in one of the windows. When he saw me, he ran off down the hill and then shied a stone at me. He is the kind who would always have stones in his pocket, ready for throwing. The stone didn't hit me, but it might have.

And all that week, every time I was alone, before school or after or at recess, he kept coming up and pestering me, wanting to know what we *did* at our secret meetings. And Gordy confided in me that Dicky had spread the rumor all through six-one-B that what we did in the secret house was play paper dolls.

It was that that decided me.

Because people can think what they like about me, and even about my paintings, but to say that I play paper dolls is a vile slander.

The next day I lay in wait for Dicky. The thing to do, I decided, was to act perfectly nice and let his own base instincts lure him to his destruction.

So I was lurking on the schoolhouse corner that morning when his horrible high school friends let him out of their jalopy. And the minute I saw him I sang out,

> "Dicky LeBaron, Dicky LeBaron,
> Put his mother's old false hair on!"

Because the only way to start a conversation with Dicky is to descend to his level. With anyone else you would make friends by being friendly, but with Dicky LeBaron's kind you have to speak their language.

Sure enough, he came swaggering right over to me in his hateful motorcycle jacket and said,

> "Lydia Green, Lydia Green,
> Bopped her Grammaw on the bean!"

And we were off to a good start.

"I hear," I said, "that you claim I play paper dolls."

"Well?" he sneered. "Don't you? What *do* you play, then, in that old hut? I know. Post office, I bet. 'Oh Gordy, Gordy, kiss my left eyebrow!'" And he fell back against a bush in a mock faint.

"I wouldn't stoop to it," I told him. "Post office is for snerds."

"All right, what *do* you do, then?" he said. "Prob'ly nothing at all, if you ask me. You just pretend it's secret so people'll think you're important!"

"A lot you know!" I said, acting indignant. "If I were to tell you what we do, you'd wither away on the spot. But no, I don't dare. Your feeble brain couldn't stand it."

"Aw, come on. Tell!" He forgot to sound tough and bullying and just sounded curious. "I'll let you wish on my rabbit's foot if you do." Honestly, you'd think he thought he was Huckleberry Finn or something.

Goodness knows, I didn't want to touch his old rabbit's foot, but I did. It felt awful. I didn't wish on it, though. I was afraid it would disagree with the real magic. Any magic of Dicky LeBaron's would probably be black as the ace of spades. I pretended to wish, and then I handed the rabbit's foot back and lowered my voice and looked around as if I were afraid somebody might overhear.

"If you want to know," I said, "we raise ghosts. That's what we do. That house is haunted."

"Yah! As if I'd believe that."

"I don't care whether you believe it or not. It's true," I said. "I'll swear on a stack of Bibles!"

I was not telling a lie, really, because we *did* have a conversation with a ghost in the secret house one day. Or at least we think we did. And besides, my fingers were crossed.

Dicky was looking at me now as if he'd like to believe me but couldn't, quite.

"All right, come and see for yourself," I said. "Come today at four o'clock." That would give us an hour to get ready for him.

He hesitated. Then he grinned, not his usual sneer but a real grin. "All right, maybe I will," he said. Suddenly he slapped me on the back. "You know, you're not so bad after all." And he went swaggering into the school.

I felt guilty after that. But I concentrated on how awful Dicky was usually, and made my plans. I decided not to tell the others just yet, though. Laura would be sure to begin preaching if she knew. And James's and Kip's idea of dealing with Dicky would be to use their fists. And I aimed to strike deeper, to his very core.

I decided the best thing to do was call a secret meeting, but not say why till the last minute. So in class that afternoon I held up one finger in the secret sign. But when we all met in the school yard, it turned out there were complications. James and Kip had football and Gordy and Deborah had promised to call on Sylvia. And Laura was due at a meeting of the Girls' Sewing Club, which she belongs to for some reason. I would sooner die.

They all promised to come to the secret house, though, as soon as their social obligations would permit. I didn't tell them who else was coming. If the magic wanted me to handle it alone, so be it. But Laura suspected.

"You've got a look in your eye," she said. "You're planning something. Remember what I warned you."

"It's my turn for the magic, isn't it?" I said. "Go to your old sewing club. But you'd better sew quick unless you want to miss everything." And I boarded the school bus. From the look on Laura's face I think she almost jumped on after me. But it was too late.

I rode to the red house and made my wish on the well and then I started for the house in the woods. But I didn't feel quite so sure of things as I climbed the last lap of the way. The sun was behind the trees already and the woods felt gloomy and cold. And I suddenly thought, what if Dicky weren't so taken in as he seemed? What if he had come early and brought cohorts, to ambush me on the way? Enemies might be hiding behind each tree right now. But when I turned to look, none jumped out.

And when I finally opened the front door of the secret house, no one was lurking there, either. So I began arranging my welcome for Dicky. By the time I'd finished, I felt pleased with myself again. I was only sorry the others weren't there to congratulate me.

My arrangement was very simple. That was its classic beauty.

In the front hall floor of the secret house there is a square hole that was once the shaft of a furnace that isn't there anymore. It is quite a big hole and dangerous; so we keep a big chest pushed over it, just in case.

It was the work of a moment to shove the chest away and turn it at right angles, to block the rest of the hall. And then I put a little rug over the hole.

So that when you-know-who opened the door in the murky misty twilight, he would naturally step right on you-know-what and fall straight down you-know-where.

But first I dropped a lot of old sofa pillows down

the shaft, beause I didn't want anybody, even you-know-who, to break an actual bone.

My plan was that I would hold Dicky prisoner in the cellar at the bottom of the shaft and haunt him and make ghost noises till he was scared and undermined, and then when the others came, we would tell him all about himself and how awful he was, and not let him out till he begged and confessed and promised to reform. It would do him a lot more good than fists, and be more lasting, too, I thought.

That was my plan.

But do you remember when you were little and you made a booby trap for someone and then went away and left it, how often as not it was you yourself who forgot and came through that door later and brought the water down on your own head and the pail, too, half the time?

You would not think a thing like that could happen to a person old enough to be in six-one-A, would you? Well, it can.

Because first I thought I would watch for Dicky from the upstairs front windows, where there's a better view. And then I got interested in the shapes of the pine trees in front of the house and thought I'd make a drawing of them. And then I was so busy drawing that I didn't hear Dicky come through the woods till he was almost at the front door. And *then* I went running downstairs in the almost darkness, and dodged round the chest in my headlong haste, and stepped right in the middle of the little rug.

And you know what happened.

The pillows at the bottom of the shaft did their duty and I found myself unkilled. But I had fallen with my leg under me, and when I tried to straighten it, my ankle felt like a thousand knives stabbing, and I could still wiggle my toes, so I thought it probably wasn't broken, but I was sure it was strained or sprained or both.

I remembered Laura's warning, and I knew the magic was up to its old tricks, teaching moral lessons again. And it was then that I heard Dicky LeBaron come up on the front stoop.

He hesitated. Of course I couldn't see him hesitating, but I could feel it. Then I heard him cautiously, creepily, creakingly open the front door.

Now was my chance, moral lessons or not. "Beware," I said, making my voice deep and ghostly. "Dicky LeBaron, your time has come."

I heard Dicky gasp. Then he must have summoned up superhuman courage. Because I heard his footsteps come closer to where the yawning hole gaped.

I waited till his head showed, and then I made the worst face I could and uttered a low moan. The way my ankle felt made that part easy. But I didn't find out till later that what with the shaft's having once led to a coal cellar, my face and hands were covered with coal dust and black as a hobgoblin's. And that helped.

Dicky took one look and let out a yell. I heard him scramble to his feet and run out of the house and jump from the stoop. And then I heard voices outside.

"What you doing round here, Dicky boy?" said the first voice. "Playing with the goody-goodies?"

"What'd you run away from us for, Dicky boy?" said the second voice. "Didn't you know we'd follow you?"

I knew those voices. It was Dicky's horrible high school friends. But they didn't sound as friendly with him as I'd have expected them to. I began to wonder if maybe when they were alone with him and didn't have anybody else to bully, they bullied *Dicky*.

"It's haunted. There's a ghost in the cellar," I heard Dicky gasp out.

"What d'you take us for, Dicky boy?" said the first high-schooler. "You think we'd believe a thing like that?"

"You trying to get rid of us, Dicky boy?" said the other. "Don't you want us to meet your high-toned friends?"

"All right, see for yourselves," Dicky said.

There were heavy footsteps now, and a second later three faces looked down the hole. "Beware," I started to say again. But my ankle was really throbbing now, and maybe that's why my voice cracked and went up high.

"That's not a ghost," said the first high school boy.

"That's a girl," said the second one.

"It's that crazy Lydia Green," said the first one.

"Gee. It *is* Lydia Green," said Dicky.

"Poor Dicky boy. Scared by a girl," said the second high school boy tauntingly.

"Aw, I was not. I knew it all along," was the vain boast of Dicky.

But the first (and worst) high school boy was smiling a mean smile. He is called Stinker, by the way, which shows what even his friends must think of him. "Well," he said, "I guess we've just about got her where we want her, haven't we?"

"I guess we have," said the second one. He is known as Smoko. Cigarettes are his life's blood. "Now we've got her what'll we do with her?"

"Let's see," said the one called Stinker. "She's the one hit me with that apple, too. Nobody does that to me and gets away with it."

"We could drop red-hot pennies down," suggested Smoko.

"Or burn up the place with her in it," said Stinker.

"You wouldn't do that, would you?" said Dicky LeBaron, sounding scared that they might.

Of course I knew they wouldn't. But even if they could talk about it, it showed what kind they were. And in my craven cowardice I said the wrong thing.

"You'd better leave me alone," I said. "I've got friends, and they're on their way here right now."

"They are?" said the one called Stinker. "That's dandy. We can wait for them and mom them when they come in the door."

I was sorry I'd spoken. Because if James and Kip got there first, they could take care of themselves, and even Laura and Gordy are spunky. But what about Deborah?

"Listen," I said. "You don't want to do that. One of them's just a little girl."

"You don't say?" said Stinker. "A little girl, huh?"

"A little *bittle* girl," said Smoko.

"Prob'ly a rich little girl, too," said Stinker.

"Gently nurtured," agreed Smoko.

"Whaddaya say we kidnap her for ransom?" said Stinker.

It was my turn to say, "You wouldn't do that, would you?" And I found an unexpected ally.

"I don't want any part of it," Dicky LeBaron surprisingly said.

"You don't?" said the Stinker one, sounding dangerously smooth and smiling.

"No I don't," said Dicky. "Picking on little girls is for creeps. And I don't like Lydia Green and she may have played a dirty trick on me, but that's my business. Why don't you scram outa here and leave her alone?"

The two high school boys came up one on each side of Dicky. Their smiles were broader and their eyes meaner than ever.

"Listen, Dicky boy," said the one called Stinker. "We let you tag along after us. Strictly for laughs, see? But we're not taking orders from squirts like you, see?"

"I don't care. I'm not going to let you hurt some little girl," said Dicky. "See?" he added.

There was a silence.

"Smoko," said Stinker, "we're going to have to do something about Dicky boy."

"Stinker," said Smoko, "you're right. A squirt like him could gum up the works."

Suddenly all three heads disappeared and there was the sound of a scuffle. And then I heard the Stinker one say, "If you like teacher's pets so much, stay and get to know them better."

And he and his friend lifted Dicky LeBaron up and dropped him right down the shaft on top of me. I saw him coming in time to brace myself. And then I heard the other two start pushing the big chest over the opening in the floor, and all was blackness.

Dicky didn't say anything for several seconds. I guess he had the wind knocked out of him. I know I had.

"Your foot's in my eye," I told him, when I could talk.

He moved it quickly. "Pardon *me*, I'm sure! I wouldn't touch your old eye with a ten-foot pole if I'd known!"

I was sorry he felt like that. Goodness knows, I'd always felt the same way about *him,* up till today, but he had shown a different side, standing up to those goons.

So I said, "Thanks for sticking up for us."

He snorted. "Don't worry, it wasn't on your account. There're just some things I draw the line at, that's all."

"I'm sorry I played a trick on you," I said. But he was still sulky.

"It was a dirty trick. I thought we were friends."

"Well, who started it? Who kept pestering us? Who threw a stone at who?" Which wasn't grammar but was the truth all the same.

"Aw, I just wondered what you all were doing, that's all. I'm sorry now I ever came near your old house."

"If you wanted to be friends with us, why not say so in the first place?" It was a new idea to me that somebody like Dicky LeBaron might feel left out of things. I'd always thought people like Dicky *wanted* to be out of things so they could jeer at them. It was a new idea to me that maybe they didn't have any choice.

"Forget it," he said shortly. "We got no time for

conversation. We got to look out for that little girl. Gimme a leg up."

I tried, but my ankle wouldn't bear my weight, let alone his.

"It's no use," he said, after a second. "Even if I could reach, I couldn't move that chest, not from here. I couldn't get any purchase. Let's see your foot."

By now we were getting used to the darkness. There was a little grating up near the ceiling that was too small for squeezing through, but it did let in a feeble glimmer, enough for Dicky to take a look at my ankle.

"Whew," he said, when he saw it. But he tore strips off his shirttail and bound it up. When he'd finished, it still hurt, but I could stand, and even hobble a little.

The grating let in sound from outside, too, and what I heard now was a familiar crashing and swishing and a high childish prattle, coming nearer. And I knew it was just as I'd feared, and Gordy and Deborah were arriving at the secret house first.

"Look out! Keep away!" I called, but it was too late.

There was a cry of triumph from the fiendish high school boys and a cry of surprise and alarm from

Gordy and Deborah, followed by a thud of blows and a scrobbling sound.

And then there was silence.

Dicky and I looked at each other. Of course we knew the two high school boys weren't really deepdyed kidnappers and it was all just a game to them, but Deborah was little and wouldn't understand and would be terrified.

"I've got to get out there," Dicky muttered.

He ran round exploring the dark passages and bumping into things, with me limping after. The house has a cellar door, the slanting kind little kids like to slide down, but when Dicky tried it, it wouldn't budge.

"Somebody's piled rocks on it," he said.

And I knew the humiliation of poetic justice, because I was the one who'd done that in my idle folly, plotting my trap for Dicky. But I will never tell him.

But then Dicky found where the chimney comes down into the cellar, and there was a hole in one side of it where the smoke pipe from the old furnace must have joined on, in olden days. We stood looking at it.

"Do you suppose?" I wondered.

"I kind of think maybe," he said.

"Chimney sweeps used to do it," I said. "Like Tom in *The Water Babies.*"

"Who?" he said. But he didn't stay for an answer. He took off one of his motorcycle boots and started knocking at the brickwork with it. He is proud of those motorcycle boots, too, but he was getting this one all scuffed and dusty. One or two bricks did come away, but it was slow work.

"Darn that magic," I said. "You'd think at least it could loosen the mortar!"

"What do you mean, magic?" said Dicky. And while he worked, I told him about the well. But he wouldn't believe a word of it.

"I bet," he said. "Some magic! About as magic as that old ghost you were telling me about!"

It is funny about some people. Dicky believed in his rabbit's foot and black cats and not walking under ladders, but real magic was a closed book to him. And I didn't have time to convince him just then because the hole in the chimney was getting big enough to try crawling into; so I boosted him up. It was a tight fit. His shoulders were the worst.

But he stretched his arms high and tried to find a hold inside the flue, and I pushed his feet from beneath. Inch by inch he began to worm his way upward.

"How is it?" I called.

"I'm getting there," he said. But he complained that he was rubbing off pounds of him on the way. Then later he called down that his front part had reached where the flue from the parlor fireplace joined the chimney and it was roomier now. "Only something's blocking the way, up above," he said. After that I couldn't hear him anymore.

But I heard something else, and it chilled my blood. Stealthy footsteps sounded in the hall overhead, and a furtive whisper.

"Psst," it said. "Anybody there?"

"No, nobody," came a second whisper. "Where'll we put the ransom note?"

Just then one of Dicky's feet must have slipped. Because a whole lot of soot came down the chimney onto me. And some must have fallen in the parlor fireplace, too, because I heard the boy called Smoko call out, "Cheesit! There *is* a ghost!"

But Stinker was made of sterner stuff.

"That's no ghost," he said. "That's somebody up the chimney. It's that squirt of a Dicky. He'll get away and ruin everything. Whaddaya say we climb up on the roof and mom him when he comes out?"

I heard the front door bang and then I heard feet on the roof shingles. I tried to call a warning up the flue to Dicky, but I knew he would never hear. There was too much of him between his ears and me.

It is awful to know horrible things are happening and have to wait and not do a thing about them. And it is even worse when the horrible things are all your fault in the first place. All I could do was hobble over near the grating in the wall and stand under it and listen. And while I listened, in my mind I begged the well to forget that other wish I'd made about getting even with Dicky and *do* something.

Or if the well had had its fill of me, and I'd be the last to blame it if it had, maybe there was some magic still left over in the secret house, and *it* would help.

And I guess the house heard me.

Because the next thing *I* heard was Stinker's voice. "I see his head," he said. "No, it's not. It's something blocking the way. I've got a grip on it, though."

The instant after that I heard a yell and the sound of someone falling off a roof. And then the sound of someone tumbling after, and more yells and running feet. It seems to me now I heard a buzzing sound, too, but Dicky says I couldn't have. And James says that is *argumentum post facto,* which is Latin, and a common phenomenon, which is just James showing off.

All I know is that I waited in wondering darkness for what seemed like hours, and then at last I heard steps in the hall and someone pushed the chest away. It was Dicky, and he was laughing. And when he told me what had happened, I knew the magic in the house had answered my prayer.

What he was laughing at was the sight that had greeted him when he finally emerged on the roof. What he had seen was Stinker and Smoko running down the hill and yelling and jumping and beating

at themselves while around and upon them a cloud of hornets nibblingly preyed.

Because the thing in the chimney had been the hornets' ancestral home, and Stinker had pulled it right out. And if that wasn't the house answering my prayer and producing magic right out of itself at just the right time, I'd like to know what it was! I couldn't convince Dicky about that, though. He said it was just hornet nature.

Dicky had a few random stings from some hornet homebodies that were still clinging to the old neighborhood when he passed by, but otherwise he was unharmed, save for scraped places and soot. He handed down a chair for me to stand on and helped me out of the cellar and out onto the stoop. A distant yelling was all that remained of Stinker and Smoko, and now it died on the breeze.

"Good riddance," said Dicky.

"I thought you liked them," I said.

"Not much," he said. "They didn't like me much either. They just wanted somebody to order around, mostly. I guess at first it made me feel big, going around with a couple of big wheels. Then I guess it got to be a habit. Now I guess maybe I broke it."

For the first time he smiled at me, sort of a

sheepish grin, and I smiled back. Then we remembered Deborah, and we stopped smiling and started searching.

The first thing we heard was a guggling noise, and the first thing we found was poor Gordy, scrobbled and gagged and tied to a tree. A bruise on his cheek bore witness that his spirit had been willing, no matter how otherwise the flesh.

And the spirit was still in him, because when I got him untied he thought at first Dicky was one of the kidnap gang and started for him with both fists.

Dicky held him off with one hand, his arms harmlessly windmilling, while I explained to him and soothed him. And just as he was getting calmer, Laura and James and Kip came plodding up the hill together and the boys thought Dicky was beating Gordy up and jumped on him, and there were more windmilling arms that I had to limp through and untangle before I could start explaining all over again.

"I told you so" were the words of Laura when she learned how my adventure had panned out. And when she heard about Deborah, her righteous fury knew no bounds.

"If anything's happened to my little sister," she said to me, "I'll never forgive you."

I felt guiltier than ever, but Dicky spoke up. "I don't think they'd actually hurt her. And they couldn't have taken her far. They didn't have time."

So then all five of us began scouring the woods to find where the hapless victim lay helplessly stashed.

It was Dicky who heard a murmuring drone, and he signaled to us, and we came up and all of us found her together. The luckless kidnappers had tied her hand and foot and left her in a hollow tree. She seemed quite happy there, playing one of her mysterious games and talking to herself.

"I am a baby squirrel," she was saying. "Soon mother squirrel will come and feed me nuts."

We untied her and plied her with questions and felt her all over for broken bones while she squirmed and giggled with utter ticklishness.

"Were the bad boys mean to you?" said Laura. "Did they scare you?"

Deborah considered. "No," she said finally. "They were quite nice." She is too young to have any taste, as yet. But Laura smothered her with sisterly hugs, all the same.

"You poor thing, it must have been awful."

Deborah freed herself. "I liked it," she said. "I was a baby squirrel."

The boys and Laura still seemed suspicious of Dicky, even after I'd told them all he had done, and Dicky was standoffish with *them*. But he and Deborah got along fine. She took his hand and talked to him about baby squirrels all the way home. Dicky had once trained one as a pet; so they had a lot in common.

But James gave me a meaningful look as the others started down the hill, and I waited with him and we brought up the end of the procession.

"What about this Dicky?" he said.

"What about him?" I said.

"Well, gee." James looked troubled. "I guess he behaved better than you'd expect, but look at the way he's always been before! Do we have to have him be one of us now?"

"I don't know about *you*," I told him. "He's my friend from now on."

"Well, sure," pursued James, "but how *much* of a one? Gordy's worked out fine, but if we keep reforming hopeless characters and adding them on, that well's going to get awfully crowded."

"You make me sick," I said. "How can people with disadvantages ever improve if the people *with* the advantages keep shutting them out?"

"That's so," James admitted. "But gee, the way he

looks! Maybe if he'd do something about that jacket and those boots?"

James can be awfully stuffy at times. But when we got to the red house, he behaved very well. He went up to Dicky and held out his hand. "That was a good job you did today," he said. "I hope from now on you'll feel free to stop by and see us anytime."

Dicky was busy spitting on his scuffed motorcycle boot and trying to polish it. "That's all right," he said. "Don't mention it." But he shook hands with James, and with Kip, too.

Gordy was hanging back and looking awkward, the way he so easily can. Dicky went up to him.

"I guess I've been kind of rough on you some-times in school, kid," he said. "No hard feelings?"

"Sure. Gee. No!" Gordy beamed with his usual forgiving toothiness.

And then Laura, ever warmhearted and carried away by the emotion of the moment, started telling Dicky all about the well and the magic and the secret meetings and the Well-Wishers' Club, and invited him to join.

But James needn't have worried about that. Because Dicky listened to it all politely. And then he shook his head.

"I guess not," he said. "No offense meant, but it sounds kind of childish to me. Thanks all the same. I'd better be moseying along now."

He ducked his head at the others and chucked Deborah under the chin. Then he winked at me and grinned.

"So long, kid," he said. "I'll be seeing you."

And he flicked a speck of dust from his motorcycle jacket and went swaggering up the road.

Six pairs of eyes followed him. And everybody seemed to like him better suddenly, now that he'd turned down our generous offer.

"You're right," said James to me. "He's not a bad kid."

"And even if he won't join the club," said Laura, "if we're ever working on a big important wish, I think he'll be useful to have handy. I think he'll help us if we ask him."

"Sure he will," I said. And it turned out we were right.

Because it turned out that there was and we did. And he did. But what the important wish turned out to be, and what we did about it, is another story.

And the beginning of that story belongs to Kip.

5

Kip Carries On

This is Kip telling the story now. The reason this part of it belongs to me is that I was the only one of us in church that Sunday.

Not that James and Laura and Deborah don't usually come, but that morning their father had forgotten to set the alarm clock. That would have been a mere nothing to me. I can always make myself wake up exactly when I want to. I do it by concentrating before I go to sleep.

But James and Laura have never been able to work that trick. I think they let other thoughts creep in, which you must never do.

As for Gordy, his mother makes him go to a different church, a big rich one in the village.

But the rest of us like the little old-fashioned country church nearby better, at least Laura and James and Deborah and I do. Lydia says she doesn't need

organized religion, and that a person can pray anywhere. This is true, I know, because I have prayed in
some peculiar places, like the time I was painting the
house and nearly fell off the roof. But for me, church
helps.

So there I was that Sunday morning, not thinking anything but church thoughts, and certainly not
about the magic or expecting an adventure to begin.
And then Mr. Chenoweth, our minister, came to that
part of the service when he makes announcements.

Only today he didn't talk about the vestrymen's
meeting or the choir or the Young People's Club. He
took off his spectacles and looked at the congregation. Then he said, "What I have to tell you today is
not church business. Or perhaps it is."

And he went on to say that he had heard of a family that was about to move into the neighborhood.
"I think some of you may know the one I mean,"
he said. And he gave the congregation another long
look.

I don't remember his exact words after that. But
what they amounted to was that some people apparently didn't want this family to move in. They didn't
want it so much that they were getting up a petition
about it. Mr. Chenoweth did not say why.

But he said, "This does not seem to me to be Christian behavior. So I myself have drawn up a statement *welcoming* these new arrivals to our community. Those who wish to sign it with me may do so after the service. Or it will be in my study at the rectory at any time. And now let us join in singing the One Hundred and Thirty-third Psalm."

If you do not know that psalm, it is the one that begins, "Behold how good and how pleasant it is for brethren to dwell together in unity."

And then Mr. Chenoweth preached a sermon on the text, "Love thy neighbor." I thought he said some pretty good things. But all the time he was saying them, there was a buzzing undertone of people talking to each other, which is something I would know better than to do during a sermon. And yet it was grown-ups who were doing it.

After church Mr. Chenoweth was waiting by the door, the way he always is, except that today there was a little desk there, too, with a paper on it. Some people were already lined up, waiting to sign the paper, and my father and mother got in line and told me to go wait in the car and see if Alice, our dog, was all right.

I knew that was just an excuse. Because Alice was

sure to be fine. She would be perfectly happy sitting in a car for a week if she thought somebody would take her for a ride at the end of it. But I walked to the car all the same, and found her peacefully sleeping, the way I knew I would. Then I came back and waited by the church door and watched the people.

Some of them were joining the line to sign the paper, but there were a lot more who stalked right out without even speaking to Mr. Chenoweth. Some of these gathered in a knot in front of the church, and I couldn't help overhearing what they were saying.

"Doesn't know his place," one lady sniffed, tossing her head. "He's entitled to his own opinion, but . . . !"

"You're right, Adele," said another. "And to bring it up in a church service, too! I think it's time we changed to the other church, with the people who count!"

"Or changed ministers!" said the first lady.

"We're going to have a fight on our hands, Harry," one man was saying.

"What if we do?" said his friend. "It's for the good of the neighborhood. Once one gets in they'll all come. We have to draw the line."

But nobody said what was wrong with the new family, or what line it was that had to be drawn.

I asked my parents about it on the way home, but I couldn't get anything out of them, either.

"I don't want to discuss it," my mother said. "It makes me too angry." But the minute we were in the house she was on the phone, telling James and Laura's mother all about it, only mysteriously; so I couldn't glean a single fact.

Parents can be maddening at times. Though mine are quite nice, as a rule.

Something was in the air and I wanted to get at the bottom of it. So I changed out of my church clothes and walked down Silvermine Road to the red house.

Laura and Lydia and Deborah and James were already assembled in the front yard, and I told them about Mr. Chenoweth and what they'd missed by missing church. In the middle of it Gordy's mother's limousine drove up and Gordy jumped out, followed by the sound of his mother's voice telling him to be careful of his Sunday suit. The things that boy has to put up with! So then I had to start over again.

"What's the matter with these people who want to move here?" said James when I'd finished. "Are they escaped criminals or something?"

"Probably moral lepers," said Lydia.

"What's a moral leper?" said Deborah.

I hurried on before anyone could tell her because once she learns a new word she uses it without mercy.

"No," I said. "I don't think it's anything like that. I think it's something else." Because I was beginning to think I knew what it might be.

"You mean it's just snobbishness, more?" said Laura.

"Sort of," I said.

"But that's terrible," said Gordy.

"Yes," I said, "it is. That's why I think we all ought to go over to Mr. Chenoweth's in a body right now and sign that paper; That's if children *can*."

"Why bother with papers?" said Lydia. "What's the magic for if not for a time like this?"

"It could be the big good turn the well's been working up to," agreed Laura.

"If it is, Kip ought to be the one in charge," said James. "Because he found out about it, and he hasn't had an adventure of his own yet." Which was generous of him, because neither had he.

"I thought of that," I admitted, "but I don't know. Mr. Chenoweth seems to have it pretty well in hand already. And I don't know whether church and magic go together."

Laura's face fell. "I never thought of that," she said. "They *don't* seem to have much in common."

There was a pause.

"What about the Witch of Endor?" Deborah spoke up suddenly. "We had her in Sunday School."

"That's right," said James. "Solomon went to see her, and *he* was holy."

"Wise, too," said Gordy. "If he could use magic, why can't we?"

"Out of the mouths of babes again," said Lydia, patting Deborah on the head.

"Well, maybe," I said. "But before we go stirring up the well, I think we ought to clear it with Mr. Chenoweth."

So we started for the rectory, walking because it isn't far and it was a fine sunny day.

When we got there, Mr. and Mrs. Chenoweth were already finishing dinner, though it wasn't one o'clock yet. Still, I imagine preaching sermons must be famishing work.

They seemed surprised to see us, but cordial. Mrs. Chenoweth offered us some store butterscotch pudding, which we civilly refused.

"We won't keep you a minute," I said. "We just want to sign that paper you talked about in church, if children are allowed to."

Mr. Chenoweth's face took on an odd expression. But he seemed to be pleased. "It so happens," he said, "that the family I have in mind includes three children. I think it would be very appropriate if the children in this neighborhood joined in welcoming them. In fact, you have given me an idea. I believe I will begin a second page, especially for children's signatures."

And he did, and we all signed it with a will.

"If you have any friends who would like to add their names to yours," Mr. Chenoweth said, "just send them to me."

I hesitated. "We do have some friends we were thinking of," I told him, "but they're not children, mostly." And I went on then about the magic and the Well-Wishers' Club and the good turns we had done so far.

"The well hasn't failed yet," I said, "and we wanted to use it now but we weren't sure. Would magic mix with church?"

"Or would it be sacrilege or something?" said Laura.

"Or just plain butting in?" said James.

Mr. Chenoweth was silent. But he was smiling to himself. Then he cleared his throat. "Ahem. I'm afraid I have not had a great deal of experience with magic. At least not the kind that lives in wells. But from what you tell me of the particular magic power you wield, I should say that it would 'mix with church,' as you put it, quite satisfactorily. I could even wish at times that more of my congregation were similarly gifted." He sighed. Then he smiled again. "In fact, I believe I may find a word of advice for you *here*. One so often can." And he took down a large Bible from a shelf and leafed through the pages. "Ah yes. Here we have it. Proverbs five: sixteen. 'Let thy fountains be dispersed abroad.'"

"And if that doesn't give us an absolutely free hand," said Lydia a minute later as we were walking home, "I'd like to know what would. We can disperse the well's magic anywhere we want to."

"Our carte is blanche," agreed James.

A minute later we arrived at the red house and all stood around the well in a solemn circle, while I spoke the words.

"Help us help that family to move in, please," I said. "And without any fuss or trouble."

And then we went inside, because time was passing and we were beginning to regret the butterscotch pudding. While we were raiding the red house's icebox, we heard familiar voices at the other end of the hall; so James and Laura led the way and we went into the living room, taking the cold chops and other things we'd found with us.

It turned out that my mother and father had stopped by and were deep in discussion with James and Laura's parents. What they were discussing I leave you to guess. When my mother saw us, she said, "Oh dear, I hate the children to hear all this."

"I think it's a good thing if they do, Margaret," said James's father. "This isn't a perfect world, and they might as well know it now."

"I think we know about it already," said James, "if the trouble's what I think it is."

"I might have known," said my mother philosophically.

"The thing that worries me," said James's father, picking up where he'd left off when we came in, "isn't getting those people moved into that house. I know we can get enough names on our side to override that petition. But there's bound to be some kind of demonstration when it happens. And how will that make the people feel about living here?"

"I know," said James's mother. "If I were they, I wouldn't want any part of this town. When I hear things like this, I wonder why I stay!"

"One reason to stay is to fix it so things like this don't happen," said my father. "Then there'll be no reason to leave. It's a problem, though, how to do it the right way."

"No it isn't," piped up Deborah suddenly. "It's all fixed. We told the well."

"Not that well again?" said my mother. And she rolled her eyes at the others. "Remember last summer?"

For our parents, unlike most parents in books, know about the magic. Or at least they know something. Though not all.

"As I think back to it," said my father, "it seems to me last summer the well did a pretty good job. When you think of the new school. And other things. On the other hand, though . . ." He broke off, looking thoughtful.

"I agree with you," said James's father.

And now all four of our parents were looking at us in that way they so often look, as though they weren't sure what we'd do next, or what they would do about it when we did.

James's father was the first to speak. "Look, kids," he said. "I know your hearts are in the right place and you want to help, but this is a pretty ticklish situation. Even with that magic you think you have, you could still go wrong. Feelings could get hurt. So if I were you, I'd stay out of it. Or if you absolutely *can't*" (and here his face relaxed in a grin, because he is an understanding man), "I'd be careful. Don't do anything rash, or drastic. Don't do anything at *all* without checking with one of us first."

"We won't," I promised. I seemed to be spokesman.

"And now back to the kitchen with those chops," said James's mother. "Honestly, Margaret, you'll think we never have a decent meal around here!"

"From the number of times Kip begs to stay to dinner here," replied my mother, "I gather you must eat a lot better than *we* do."

We left them vying in polite laughter like a couple of rival hostesses, and went back to the kitchen and put our dishes in the dishwasher and our chop bones in the garbage can. And then we went outside.

"You know, there's something in what they say,"

James said in a troubled voice. "I don't see how the magic's going to manage it without big scenes and people quarreling."

"Leave it to the well," said Laura. "It'll seek its own level."

"And while we're waiting," I said, "at least we can tell people about it. Our friends and all the Well-Wishers. So they'll be prepared for whatever happens."

This didn't seem to be rash or drastic enough to have to consult a parent about it; so we started out, taking a big sheet of blank paper with us that could be added to Mr. Chenoweth's list of names later.

We dropped in first on Lydia's grandmother. She is always a firebrand in any cause, provided she can be fighting against something. In some ways Lydia is very like her.

"I'm with you," she said, writing her signature at the top of the paper in big sprawling letters. "We'll lick the Philistines or bust." That is what she always calls anybody she doesn't agree with. I do not know why. Except that I seem to remember about the Philistines that they had the jawbones of an ass, and that is certainly true of the people who were spreading ugly talk in this case.

After that we stopped at Hopeful Hill and talked to Doctor Emma Lovely. Or rather Gordy did most of the talking because he knows her best.

"Well, well, Diogenes," she said to him when she'd heard the story. "Still looking for an honest man in a naughty world? And lo, Abou Ben Lovely's name led all the rest! Well, at least it comes second."

And she signed her name under Lydia's grandmother's, with a string of letters after it that probably meant something important and medical. "Peculiar psychology, people who want to keep other people out of things," she added. "Comes from a thwarted childhood, of course. Still, that's no excuse."

We went past Gordy's house next, but no one suggested stopping. Everyone was privately afraid it might be embarrassing for Gordy. Mrs. Witherspoon is not a person you can depend on to be on the right side, in a thing like this. So we marched straight by the driveway and no one said a word. No one looked at Gordy, either. But he was in front of me, and I couldn't help seeing the back of his neck get red.

But we talked to a lot of other people who were highly cooperative. The woman who had given us the Lady Baltimore cake not only signed the paper, but offered to bake another Lady Baltimore cake for the new arrivals as soon as they were safely moved in.

As for Miss Wilson, when we told her, her face got crosser than I've ever seen it in school. "Why must there be hate and prejudice in the world," she said, "when you think what a little love can do?" And her look softened as she gazed out of the window at Sylvia, playing in the yard.

After that we visited some of the friends we had made the summer before. Miss Isabella King, the little old lady who owns the abandoned silver mine, was gentle but peppery, as always. "This could never have happened in the old days," she said. "In *my* time, neighbors were neighborly."

Mr. Hiram Bundy, the town banker, was taking tea with her in her parlor, as he so often is. He hemmed and hawed when we asked him to sign the paper, but Miss Isabella gave him a firm look and he did it.

From Miss King's we went up the river to where the movie-starish lady and her husband live. They are the people whose long-lost heir we rescued from kidnapping one day.

When we arrived at their palatial estate, the heir's parents were just driving off in one of their collection of sports cars, probably bound for some sophisticated cocktail party. But they stopped and listened politely while I made my speech.

"Oh, Gregory," said the movie-starish lady when I'd finished, "must we be involved? We came to the country for peace."

"Peace at such a price," said the heir's father, "is the peace of ostriches. We want our son to grow up in a decent world, don't we?"

I have heard that is not true, by the way, about ostriches. I mean, about their burying their heads in the sand when danger comes. But I did not bring it up. And the heir's parents signed their names under Mr. Hiram Bundy's.

Our last stop was at Madame Salvini's house. The hedge had been clipped since we saw it last, and Mr. Adam Appledore was in the act of repainting the mailbox, while Madame Salvini stood by holding the paint can and singing "Home on the Range" softly under her breath.

"Ayeh," said Mr. Appledore, when we told him about the new family and asked him to sign the paper. "I'll put my name to that. It takes all kinds to make a world, and a good thing too. More interesting that way."

"Why not have a housewarming party for them?" said Madame Salvini. "I would be glad to sing."

"I'll see about it," I said quickly. Because I was not sure her singing would be the kind of welcome a new family would want. But I thanked her, anyway. And the housewarming party was not a bad idea.

By this time it was getting to be late afternoon and we had biked all over most of the town. And while we may have had a ham sandwich here and a plate of cookies there, we were beginning to think lovingly of dinner. Not only that, but the thought of homework loomed. So we separated for the evening. Tomorrow at school would be soon enough to get signatures from the kids we knew.

But the next day at recess we found the playground already buzzing with discussion. Because naturally the people who were against the new family's moving in had talked about it in front of their children just as our families had talked about it in front of us.

The division was about what you'd expect. The stuffy, hopeless, purseproud ones were on the wrong side as usual, and the feckless goons who'll do anything for a little excitement. All the really good kids saw the idea right away, though, and were only too happy to sign the paper.

But of course there are always the mindless ones who never have any opinion of their own and have to borrow other people's. We worked on these and got a few more names.

Only while Lydia was handing the paper round, a big bullying boob called Clarence Hindman suddenly grabbed it right out of her hand and went running across the playground with it before James or I could stop him, and yelled out that he was going to tear it up. He might have done it, too, but just then Dicky LeBaron came round the corner.

He saw James and me and the rest of us running after Clarence and stuck out his foot just in time. Clarence tripped over it and lost his balance and almost fell and *did* drop the paper, and I rescued it.

"What's the big deal, dad?" Dicky wanted to know, and we told him.

He considered for a minute. "These people want to move here and some other people are trying to stop 'em?"

"That's right," I said. "This paper's to stop them stopping them."

"I'll sign that," he said. "So will you, won't you, Clarence? And so will you and you and you." And he looked round in a masterful way at the crowd of tough little kids that follows him round and hangs on his every word. Then he licked his pencil and added his name, with a flourish under it, and where he led the others followed, even Clarence, who was looking sheepish now. Altogether it made seventeen more signatures that we wouldn't have had otherwise.

"Thanks," I said.

"Forget it, dad," Dicky said. And he strutted away.

That afternoon we took the papers, three pages of them by now, to Mr. Chenoweth. He seemed pleased but troubled. What was troubling him was the same thing that had been troubling our parents.

"With these pages added to my own list," he said, "I'm sure we have enough names to show that the majority of public opinion is on our side. But I am still afraid there may be unpleasantness."

We were still afraid, too, particularly after something Gordy learned that night. Because that night a deputation from the other side called on Mrs. Witherspoon. She is an influential person in her own circle, and these people wanted her to join them, but I'm happy to say she wouldn't. She wouldn't sign our paper (because Gordy asked her), but she wouldn't go along with the intolerant ones, either. She said it would be undignified. Which is about the best we could have expected of her, I guess, considering her background and training.

But Gordy sat on the stairs and listened to everything that was said, and was not ashamed of eavesdropping in a good cause, and reported it all back to us.

What these people were planning was to march down Silvermine Road in a group the very day the new folks moved in, and hand them a letter saying they weren't wanted and advising them to move away again, and offering to buy the house from them for exactly what they had paid for it.

"All perfectly quiet and respectable," said the chairman of the deputation. "No violence or mob stuff. Our motive is the good of the community."

"A mob is a mob," Gordy told us his mother said then, "no matter what the motive. And it is *never* respectable."

And I say good for her.

We had Gordy report his counterspyings to our parents, and what he said worried them, too.

"They'll do it, and there's not a thing we can do to stop them," said James's mother.

"What day are the people moving in?" I wondered.

"Saturday," said my mother.

"That's right," said Gordy. "This mob's going down there at three o'clock Saturday afternoon."

"Then it's up to us to figure out something before then to try to counteract it," said my father.

"*We* could all march down there in a body, too, and say we don't agree," said my mother, "but it seems like descending to their level and squabbling."

"Like two dogs fighting over a bone," said James's father. "Who would blame the bone if it moved away in disgust?"

"We'll have to think of something better," said my father.

"Or maybe the well will," said Laura.

Our parents looked at each other.

But we went and told the well this latest development and asked it to be working on it.

"We've got three days before Saturday," I said.

But the next day, Wednesday, we still hadn't thought of anything and neither, apparently, had the well. We didn't hold a secret meeting after school that day, but went our separate ways. Homework was the excuse, but I guess everybody knew everybody else wanted to be alone and think.

I decided to go for a walk, because I generally think better on my feet, and moving. Just as I was starting out, I heard a pattering sound behind me and something went, "Seep seep seep," and I knew Alice our dog had decided to come, too. "Seep seep seep," is all Alice knows how to say, except for hunting cries. She has not found out about barking as yet.

We do not see a great deal of Alice, as a general rule. She has a wonderful secret life of her own with rabbits and things, and runs round the woods all day attending to this. But once in a while she comes across one of us in the course of her wanderings, and then she is overjoyed and quite willing to walk along with me, or Mom, or Pop as the case may be, for a while, before returning to her personal concerns.

She walked along with me now, and our feet turned up Silvermine Road, in the opposite direction from the red house. I wasn't noticing particularly where I was going, but of course I was thinking about the new family and that must have guided my footsteps unbeknownst, because the next thing I knew I was staring at the house that I'd been told was the one the family was planning to move into.

It was (and is) a roomy white house of the kind that is called a saltbox, not really an old house but a good imitation of one, sitting at an angle to the road under some fine tall oak trees. It looked pleasant and peaceful and as though a family could be very happy in it, though the grounds were neglected. The lawn needed cutting and the backyard was tall with weeds. But beyond that was quite a good woods.

I stood there looking at the house and thinking about the problem and marveling at man's inhumanity to man, as the poem by Robert Burns that we had to learn at school puts it, when suddenly Alice began to bay and charged round the house and plunged through the weeds and into the woods, and I knew a rabbit must be passing by. Not that Alice has ever *caught* a rabbit, but she lives in hope that she will.

I went after her, not because I expected anything to happen, but just for something to do.

The weeds behind the house were just tall, ugly weeds, but then came a belt of big trees with a sort of opening in the middle that might have been a path or a road once but now it was all choked with brushwood. I pushed through this for a while and then I came out into a clearing. And when I saw that clearing I forgot about Alice and just stood there looking.

I am not one to go mooning on about nature, but my mother belongs to the Garden Club and her rock garden is just about her life work, so naturally I can't help knowing a little bit about plants and bushes. And even in October that clearing was something to see.

There were lots of dark purple wild asters leaning around the way they do, and bittersweet vines full of berries were twining up all the trees. And at the far end of the clearing a big bush of the kind that is called burning bush, or sometimes wahoo, with all its leaves crimson enough to be burning, all right, was standing all by itself, as if it were in charge of the whole show.

These are all wild plants and could have come there by accident. But as I looked around, I saw other things, snowberry bushes with their little white marbles, and a forsythia, not all yellow and frothy like scrambled eggs the way it would be in spring, but still I would know a forsythia any time of the year.

And when I looked closer, I saw little green points showing under it that I recognized as the leaves grape hyacinths push up in the fall. And I knew there must have been an old garden here once.

Just at that moment Alice suddenly came running back toward me, and then stopped and looked behind her. Her tail was between her legs and her ears were flat to her head and the fur at the back of her neck was rising, and she seemed to be looking at something that wasn't there.

It is funny how sometimes you don't notice it when magic begins to show. I don't think I thought of the well or our wish in that minute at all. Because Alice often acts like that. She behaved that very same way the first morning she met Lydia's grandmother, old Mrs. Green. Still, that morning was the beginning of our very first magic adventure that first summer. So it all adds up, when you look back.

But I didn't start looking back till later. Right now I was just idly curious enough to push on and see what Alice was staring at.

Beyond the burning bush I came on a big hole in the ground and a tumbled heap of fieldstones and old rotted boards with poison ivy growing over them, and I realized there must have been a house there once, back in the olden days.

And that seemed to be all.

But magic can start working in your mind whether you know it's there or not. And as I went back to the road, I began thinking of the garden that was still partly growing long after the old house had joined the dust of centuries.

And it was then that I had my idea.

Because what could be a better housewarming present than the beginning of a garden?

Kind words and good wishes are all very well, but their echo dies on the empty air. And Lady Baltimore cakes are tasty, but their taste is the thing of a moment. But a garden, if it's well made, will last longer than a man and go on and on to time immemorial, probably, when you consider seeds and what they can do in even one year.

So that if we took the new family presents of plants and shrubs, it would be a good turn and a symbol, too. It would mean not only that we were glad they were there, but that we wanted them to stay on forever, and their descendants after them.

I could hardly wait to tell the others my idea and see what they thought of it, but right now it was getting toward suppertime; so I raced Alice home and got on the telephone and called a conference for that night, at my house.

And after dinner there we all sat assembled, James and Laura and their parents and mine, and Lydia and Gordy. Even Lydia's grandmother put in an appearance, though she hardly ever goes out socially. And Deborah had been allowed to stay up and come along.

It was quite an audience to have to talk in front of, but I told my plan as quickly and simply as I could. When I'd finished, there was a silence, but not the critical-sounding kind.

"I could get the Garden Club to work on it," my mother said then dreamily. "It would make a wonderful fall project."

"Now, Margaret," said my father quickly, "leave your ladies out of this. They may be all right for getting the flowers and stuff together. But I think the children ought to do the whole presentation. They're the best weapon we have."

"We could take houseplants, too," said Laura, "so they'll have flowers indoors this winter."

"And clean up their yard for them," said James, "as a surprise."

"We can tell all the Well-Wishers," said Gordy. "They'll prob'ly all want to send things over."

"And we can get there at a half-past two on Saturday," said Lydia, "before the people on the other side have time to deliver their nasty old letter."

"Good idea," said James's father. "The sight of you ought to shame them."

"If anything could," said Lydia's grandmother.

I didn't say anything. But I knew the feeling of justified pride. Because I am not usually the one who thinks up the important, exciting ideas.

Not that I was taking all the credit for this one. It is the well and the magic that keep the good turns going, we know that. But always one of us has to be smart enough to interpret the magic and justify the ways of the well to man, and usually it is James or Laura or Lydia who does this, and Gordy and I follow along.

For the next two days we were busy. While Laura and Lydia went around spreading the news, James and Gordy and I spent most of our time at the new family's house.

First we got a fire permit from Town Hall and cut down the weeds in the backyard and burned them. Then we raked leaves into a big pile for a compost heap, which is what every young garden needs most. And then I took our power mower over, and we mowed the whole lawn.

After that I had another idea. And we borrowed Pop's chainsaw and cut down brushwood and opened up the pathway to the clearing; so that from the back of the house you could see between the trees all the way to the purple asters and the red of the burning bush. By the time we'd finished with that job we were really tired, but the place looked keen.

And now it was Friday night and the important day loomed. The response from the Well-Wishers and our other friends and our parents' friends and Mr. Chenoweth's congregation had been terrific. Everyone had promised to send or bring something.

And Saturday morning the floral offerings started to arrive, at our house because it's nearest to the new family's. And besides, this was my adventure.

There were seedlings and packages of seed and pots of flowers and baskets of flowers till our hall and living room looked like a plant nursery.

As the day wore on contributors began arriving in person.

Miss Isabella King drove up in her one-hoss shay with Mr. Hiram Bundy beside her, bringing slips from the rose called Silver Moon that grows all over her old silver mine. Mr. Bundy had already donated a thousand daffodil bulbs (and we had already planted them with aching backs under the oak trees on the new family's lawn).

The long-lost heir's father appeared in a sports

car with rare orchids from his movie-starish wife's greenhouse. Mr. Adam Appledore arrived in a truck with six young apple trees from his condemned orchard. Madame Salvini, who was with him, brought a record she had made of the "Flower Duet" from *Madame Butterfly,* taking both parts.

Miss Wilson turned up with Sylvia and an African violet that she had helped Sylvia grow herself from a leaf cutting.

Mrs. Witherspoon asserted her neutrality by remaining away, but she sent her chauffeur with a potted palm for Gordy's sake.

As for the cake-baking lady, she had already made her Lady Baltimore cake before she heard our floral plans, but she added some frosting daisies on top to tone in with the general idea.

Of all our friends and relations, I'm not sure which made the most spectacular entrance, Doctor Emma Lovely or Dicky LeBaron.

Doctor Emma came trudging down the road looking more wild-haired and windswept than usual, and draped with a collection of vines and branches and muddy roots and stems that might have been a witch's last year's castaways, but were probably the rarest of native wildflowers.

And while we were talking to her, Dicky LeBaron came up to the front door carrying the biggest pot of store chrysanthemums I had ever seen, that he must have bought with his own money.

"Gee, you shouldn't have spent all that," I said, for I was pretty sure he couldn't afford it.

"Stay cool, dad," he said. "In this case I got special reasons."

Our parents had formed a transportation committee to collect all the kids who had signed our petition at school, and now cars started arriving and discharging passengers till there wasn't a parking place to be found on either side of the street from our house all the way to the new family's. And that whole stretch of Silvermine Road began to look more like a Sunday School picnic than anything else as children of all ages milled about, cheering each new car and each new bouquet as they appeared.

Laura and Lydia tried to urge the madding crowd into parade formation, two by two with the smallest in front and everyone carrying something in bloom or at least green. But they had trouble keeping the younger children in line until Dicky LeBaron noticed this and gave a whistle.

Right away the gang of tough little kids that follows him around came running up, and Dicky detailed them to keep order. They turned out to be good at this, though not overgentle.

We had kept the whole idea of the flower shower a secret from the enemy, or tried to, but something must have leaked out, because long before three o'clock some of the anti-new-people people began driving along Silvermine Road, looking for places to leave their cars and not finding any. You could tell them by their self-satisfied expressions.

And Doctor Lovely and Lydia's grandmother, who had established themselves in our tower room with Doctor Lovely's bird-watching field glasses, reported that the Smugs, as we had begun to call these people from a book my mother was reading at the time, were parking beyond the new family's house and forming their procession up there.

I took time out for a look through the field glasses, myself. I could see the new family's house as plain as plain. I saw the moving van leave, and then the father of the new family came out and stood on his lawn and gave his house a proud, loving, owner-like look. And then I saw him stare around curiously at the activity that was going on, all up and down the road, and I thought how surprised he must be at finding such a citified traffic jam out in the middle of the country. But little did he know!

Then as I watched he went inside again, and I decided it was now or never, if we still hoped to be the earliest to arrive. So I ran downstairs and gave the order to start, and the procession got underway.

I had to admit the littlest kids looked cute, carrying their child's-size flowerpots. But it was not my idea to have them start singing "Home, Sweet Home." That was Laura. I would never have allowed

anything so mawkish. Still, maybe it wasn't a bad plan. Because there is something about the sound of infant voices raised in sugary song that can soothe the most intolerant breast. Apparently.

For I was walking along by the front of the procession, carrying a particularly fierce-looking rubber plant, and I saw and heard exactly what happened.

Just as we came abreast of the gate to the new family's front yard, about ten or twelve of the Smugs arrived from the opposite direction. I was too excited to count, but I saw their stuffy expressions and the letter in the hand of their leader.

But the children ignored them, as I'd told them to do, and went right on marching and warbling in their childish purity (and more off-key than Madame Salvini). And suddenly the leader of the Smugs stopped and cleared his throat and I heard him say, "Now that it's time, I can't do it, Harry. Not in front of those kids. It sticks in my craw."

"Maybe it wasn't such a good idea in the first place, Fred," said his friend.

And the opposition wavered and fell back and left the field in shamefaced surrender, or at least the respectable part of it did, and we marched by them and through the gate and up the front walk.

But all was not yet won.

For at that moment, from beyond the faltering Smugs, about a dozen rowdyish high school boys surged forward. Probably they had just come along to look on and jeer, but now they saw their chance. And when I recognized Stinker and Smoko among them, I was ready for the worst.

Because I could see that from their point of view the crowd of us, carrying our girlish flowers and singing our girlish song, must look like all that was sissy, not to say asinine, and a fit prey for the slings and arrows of the multitude.

Then, right while I was thinking this, I heard a whistle.

Dicky LeBaron must have seen Stinker and Smoko and their friends at the same moment I did. And at his whistle his gang of tough little kids came up on the run. I had been annoyed with them before for not carrying any of the trees or bushes and just tagging along at the end of the procession, but I realized now that Dicky must have foreseen trouble right from the start.

And just as if they'd rehearsed it, Dicky and his followers linked themselves together in a human chain between the kids in the procession and the menacing high school boys, and stood there with their heels dug in, glaring toughly and daring the world to attack.

I saw Stinker's and Smoko's hands go to their pockets and come out with rocks in them. And I saw the new people peering in a scared way from their front windows.

And then, just as I was sure big trouble was coming, a wonderful thing happened.

Because it turned out that the rumor that had spread to the high school had reached the good kids as well as the gang of bullies. And now they acted accordingly.

Before a rock could cleave the air, two stalwart youths appeared, one on each side of Stinker, and pinioned his arms. And the same thing happened to Smoko and the rest of that whole crowd. And their pointless rocks fell helpless to the ground.

Leading the rescue party was the big smiling boy called Tom Corkery, and when I saw him, my pride and relief knew no bounds.

Tom Corkery is captain of the high school baseball team and president of the student council and just about everybody's hero for miles around, and to think that he had bothered to interfere and save the day made me feel as though my adventure were pretty important. And to crown it all, he came over to me afterwards.

"This was a good idea of yours, Willoughby," he told me, Willoughby being my last name.

"Thanks, Corkery, you were a big help," I said. And we shook hands.

And that just about made my day.

And the hapless bullies were hustled away, that they could nothing common do or mean upon that memorable scene, as the poet says.

With them out of the way and no further rifts to mar life's lute, as Laura put it, we proceeded as I had planned.

We placed the rosebushes and dwarf evergreens around the lawn and the hardy perennials in the empty flower beds, as if they were already growing there. We grouped the apple trees to one side like a miniature orchard and massed the potted plants on the front steps.

When we'd finished, it looked pretty elegant, if I do say it myself, and just like a page out of *Better Homes and Gardens*. And the new family came out on the porch and stood looking around with expressions of wonder and delight.

And when Deborah saw the family, she realized for the first time why it was that the Smugs had tried to keep them from moving in.

Her voice rang out loud and clear. "Oh," she said, "is *that* all it was?"

"Yes," I told her, "that's all it was."

"Why, how perfectly silly!" said Deborah.

"Yes, wasn't it?" I said.

And I went up to the father of the family and made my best dancing-school bow. "Welcome to Silvermine Road," I told him.

"Thank you," he said. And we shook hands.

I will draw a veil over the scene that followed.

Because the mother of the family turned out to have thoughts that did not lie too deep for tears, and she cried buckets for sheer joy, and Laura joined in happily, and the youngest of the family's three children was a mere baby and when it saw the flowers it waved its arms and cooed, and we all felt sort of icky and yet noble, and if my own eyes seemed to be perspiring there for a second, why dwell on it now?

The father of the family asked us inside, and we went in for a bit, though it was rather a tight squeeze as there were sixty-three of us.

The furniture was standing around as if it didn't

feel sure it belonged there yet, the way furniture always does on moving day. But you could tell that the rooms were going to look fine when they got used to themselves. There was a piano at one end of the living room, and it developed that the father was the one who played this, and after a little persuasion he played part of the "Moonlight Sonata" and it was keen.

After that we thanked him and said good-bye and that we hoped we'd see them all again soon.

And we went home to tell our parents and the Well-Wishers all about it.

It had been such an exciting afternoon that nobody felt much like getting back to normal all the rest of that day. I asked Mom if James and Laura and Lydia and Gordy and those of our grown-up friends who wanted to could stay at our house for potluck supper and she said why not? And afterwards we played charades. Dicky LeBaron wouldn't stay, though, and I was sorry. I was getting to like him better and better.

But I found out later that there were parties that night all over town to celebrate.

What the Smugs and Stinker and Smoko did with their evening I would be the last to guess.

But even long after midnight, when everyone had gone home and I was in bed, I was still too keyed up to go to sleep. I kept going over the whole adventure in my mind. And I kept thinking about the clearing in the woods with the deserted garden and the tumbledown house, and the way I'd felt about them and the way our dog Alice had acted, and the way the magic had really begun percolating right at that minute, taking hold of my thoughts and giving me the idea of what to do.

It was so late when I finally dozed off that I almost didn't wake up in time for church. I did, though. Nearly everyone was there, including the new people. They were all smiles, except for the biggest little boy, who looked solemn.

And Mr. Chenoweth was wreathed in smiles, too, and preached a pretty good sermon on the text, "For lo, the flowers appear on the earth."

But I was impatient for next day, when Town Hall would be open. And on Monday as soon as school was out, I went straight there, to the department where they keep the old records. I had been there often before, to look up different things I was curious about. James laughs at me about this, and calls me Old Father Antiquary. But I am interested in my town and its history.

I found the deed for the new family's land and traced the ownership back, and the earliest known owner was somebody called Hagar Gryce. That was all Town Hall could tell me and it wasn't much.

But then I went to call on Miss Isabella King, as the oldest living inhabitant I knew, to see if she had ever heard of Hagar Gryce and could tell me about her. And she had and she did.

And when I heard what she had to say, I hurried to the red house where the others were waiting, and told *them*.

"You see," I was saying a few minutes later, "this Hagar Gryce was a runaway slave who was saved by the Underground Railroad. And afterwards she lived there in an old log and fieldstone cabin and grew flowers and herbs. And the country people used to come to her and said she did magic cures. So you see it all connects. What's left of her magic must be still hanging around there where her old house used to be."

"It's kind of wonderful to think of it waiting all those years for you to come by," said Gordy.

"Waiting to help just the right people move in, too," said James.

"Maybe it was the magic that called them there in the first place," said Lydia.

Only Laura looked a little disappointed. "Then this magic didn't have anything to do with the well at *all?*"

"Sure it did," I said. "All magic must be part of the same family, mustn't it? It stands to reason. I wished on the well and the well sent me on to the nearest spot it knew where the right kind of magic was to fit this particular case."

"Like switching a car on to the next station," said Lydia.

"Like the Underground Railroad!" said James.

"Sure. It all connects," I said again.

"What's an Underground Railroad?" said Deborah.

"A subway train," said James, not wanting to go into all that now.

But Laura was looking happier again.

"Anyway," said Gordy, "this was just about the most important big good-turn adventure yet, I'd say, *however* the magic managed it. When you think what it really sort of stood for, I'd say it was better than the new school one, even. Or just as good as. Whadda *you* say?"

"And now I suppose the magic's nearly over," sighed Lydia. "In books the big adventures always come just before the end."

"Hey!" said James. "It can't be, not yet. I haven't had my turn!"

"Neither have I," said Deborah.

We all laughed, because we hadn't been thinking of her as old enough to have a turn of her own. But we were wrong, as it turned out.

And Lydia was wrong about the magic being over, too. It wasn't, not by a long shot.

Even the adventure of the new family wasn't really finished. Not yet. Not quite. The new people had moved in, but they hadn't started living here yet.

It is Deborah that *that* story belongs to. Deborah and one other.

And now I'll let them tell about it in their own way.

6

Deborah Dictates

This chapter is not really what the title says it is. Not exactly.

But the thing is that Deborah asked me to put her story down in words for her. I don't know why she chose me to be the one.

At first she did try dictating it to me, but that turned out to be too slow and we weren't getting anywhere. So she said, "I'll tell you what happened and you write it out."

So that is what I am doing, exactly as she told it.

Except that I come into the story, too, a little, and when I get to that part, I'll tell you about it just as it seemed to me.

I'm not going to say who this is, writing. But maybe you can guess who I am, as the story goes on. There is a pun in the title of the chapter that will help you to do that, maybe.

You might not think I would know what a pun is, but I do. Just because I talk hep talk some of the time does not mean that I don't understand good English. And I may have had my troubles in school, with this teacher and that one, but I am not dumb. And lately I am getting to like school more and more.

But to get back to the story.

After the day we all welcomed the new people to Silvermine Road, and the big deal *that* turned out to be, you would think everything would stay real cool for the new family from then on.

But such is not always the case.

It is when the big deals are over and the ordinary daily living starts that the real test comes. Ordinary daily living is not what most people are at their best at. And that goes for just about everybody in this story. Except maybe Deborah.

Where Deborah comes into it is that the oldest of the three children in the new family turned out to be six years old. And that meant he was in the first grade, and on Wednesday of that same week when he came to school for the first time he was put in Deborah's room.

His given name turned out to be Hannibal, and that's what started the trouble, in a way. But not really. Some of it was his own fault and some of it was other people's, and some of it was just human nature I guess.

That first morning Miss Silloway, the first-grade teacher, brought him into the class and introduced him.

"Children," she said, "this is Hannibal. And we're glad to have him with us, aren't we, class?"

"Yes, Miss Silloway," said the class.

"And you're glad to be with us, aren't you, Hannibal?" said Miss Silloway.

"No," said Hannibal.

"Oh, I think you are, really," said Miss Silloway.

"No," said Hannibal.

Miss Silloway frowned, but her mouth went on smiling. "Well, then, we'll just have to *make* Hannibal glad to be with us, won't we, class?"

"Yes, Miss Silloway," said the class, but not quite so enthusiastically.

"No," said Hannibal, at the same time.

Miss Silloway stopped smiling. "Sit down, Hannibal," she said.

Hannibal sat down.

But things went on being like that all morning. Hannibal sat there solemn and silent except when

Miss Silloway called on him or asked him a question, and then he said, "No." And when recess came in the middle of the morning, he stood by himself at one end of the playground, doing nothing.

Deborah and some of the boys and girls went over to him.

"Wouldn't you like to play with us?" said Deborah.

"No," said Hannibal.

"Maybe later you will," said Deborah.

"No, I won't," said Hannibal.

"I guess maybe he'd rather be by himself at first," said Deborah to her friends. "I know how it is."

"No, you don't," said Hannibal.

"Yes, I do," said Deborah, smiling at him. And she and her friends went back to their game of tag, and left Hannibal idly kicking at the pebbles of the playground.

But all the others were not so understanding. The first, second, and third grades all have recess together, and pretty soon some of the third-graders started clustering around Hannibal and teasing him.

That is the way some people always act when a person is different. I know all about it because I have been the one who was different, in my day. That's why I was so interested in the new family in the first place, and why I spent all my money on those chry-santhemums, because I know how being different feels.

Not that I am any angel. There have been other times when somebody else has been the different one and I have gone along with the heckling majority. Like the way we used to treat Gordy, just because he was rich and toothy and no good at games. But that is over and done with.

All the same, you can see how these kids felt. Those who had been *for* the new family were disappointed that Hannibal had turned out all cross and sulky and no fun. And those who had been against could now say, "You see?" and "I told you so."

It was Hannibal's name that they picked on first.

"What did you say your name was?" said somebody. "Hannibal or Annabelle?"

Hannibal mumbled something.

"What did he say?" said somebody else.

"He said Annabelle, didn't you, Annabelle?" said a horrid little girl with corkscrew curls called Mabel Timkin, whose father was one of the Smugs who hadn't wanted the new family there in the first place. "'Good gracious, Annabelle!'" she cried, dancing around Hannibal. "'Good gracious, Annabelle!'"

And others took up the cry.

"'Good gracious, Annabelle!'" they yelled. "Oh, Annabelle, say not so!"

And Mabel Timkin shrilled out, "Chase me, chase me, Annabelle; I've never been chased before!"

Hannibal stood this a long time and then he let out a roar. "All right!" he said. "I'll chase you and I'll catch you and kill you!" And he ran after Mabel Timkin and grabbed her by her corkscrew curls and pulled. And Deborah, who was watching, admits that she was glad he did. Mabel Timkin had asked for it.

But of course all that really did for Hannibal was give the meaner kids more of an excuse to pick on him. And now some of the boys started circling round him in a menacing way and saying, "Fighting with a girl, Annabelle? That's bad, Annabelle. We'll have to teach you better, Annabelle." And one of them got a willow switch and started hitting at Hannibal's legs, not really hard but hard enough to sting.

Hannibal stood there in the middle of the circle, hopping from one leg to the other to keep away from the switch, and tears slowly and silently started coming down his cheeks. And it was then that Deborah went running to find me.

The reason I was there in the first place is that I have just lately been made monitor of the playground during little kids' recess. I know why Miss Wilson did it. She has some crazy theory that if I'm given more responsibility, it may bring out the best in me. But I can see through her. Though I do not mind the job really, now I am used to it.

Anyway, there I was, teaching a lot of dumb second-graders to play Red Rover, Red Rover, when Deborah came running up to me, all excited.

"Come quick," she said. "It's Hannibal."

And I followed her.

When they saw me coming, the mean kids melted away, because my word is law on that playground, if I do say it myself.

But of course I didn't know what all had been happening till Deborah told me later. So I got the whole thing wrong. I thought it was the kids who wouldn't play with Hannibal. I didn't know it was Hannibal who wouldn't play with the kids.

So I looked around for one of my little brothers.

Little brothers are one thing I always have plenty of, there being nine kids in my family. And three of them are in the lower grades. The first one I saw now was the second-grade one, who is called Pete. And I whistled him over.

"Okay," I said to him and Hannibal when I had them standing together. "Now play."

"Do I hafta?" said Pete.

"No," said Hannibal.

"You'll play," I said, "or else. You'll play or I'll knock your heads together."

"No, I won't," said Hannibal.

"Don't, then. No skin off my neck," said Pete. And he ran back to his gang.

I felt Deborah tugging at my jacket. "That's not the way," she said. She is smart for her age.

Because I could see that it wasn't. There was more here than met the eye.

I squatted down by Hannibal. "Look, dad," I said. "Let's get this straight. The kids want to be your friends. But they can't do it all by themselves. *You* have to do some of it."

"I'm not your dad," said Hannibal. "And they're not my friends. They don't want me. They tried to keep me out. Well, I don't want them. I didn't want to be here in the first place. I want to go back to New York."

This was the longest speech he had made yet, and I began to think I was getting somewhere. At least I had started him talking. And I knew now what the trouble was.

"We didn't try to keep you out," I said. "We helped you move in. Remember?"

"Flowers," said Hannibal. "Who needs flowers? You didn't do it for us. You did it for yourselves. So you'd feel good."

Hannibal was pretty wise for his age, too. Maybe *too* wise. Maybe there had been things in his life already that made him that way.

I knew just how he felt, too. Sort of the way I used to feel when the social worker used to come round our house, prying and asking questions and talking about underprivileged children and all with the best intentions, of course. But he had it wrong.

"Okay, Hannibal," I said. "So you didn't want to come here. But you *are* here, so why not make the best of it? Suppose you play with Deborah now, just to show you can."

And then all of a sudden Hannibal seemed to go wild.

"Play!" he said scornfully. "Play! All right, I'll play! I'll play tag. You're it." And he butted me in the stomach with his head, there where I was squatting, and knocked me back off my heels. "And you're it!" And he gave Deborah a push that sent her staggering. And then he went running all over the playground, yelling at the top of his voice and pushing just about everybody.

And at that moment the bell rang and recess was over.

I made sure Hannibal went back in the school building with the others, and that was all I could do just then. I had to get back to class.

But I thought about Hannibal a lot the rest of that day.

I know that there are times when being mean and ornery seems to be the only way out. Like that year I felt poor and out of things and against everybody, and went around knocking down mailboxes and destroying property.

Eventually you learn that knocking things down doesn't do a bit of good. Or knocking people down, either. But sometimes it takes a while to find this out.

Deborah told me later that Hannibal was just plain awful in class after recess and in the afternoon, answering Miss Silloway back and hitting out at the other kids and throwing his books on the floor. The

171

children of the Smugs were saying "I told you so" worse than ever. And even some of the good boys in the class vowed that as soon as school was over they were going to get Hannibal.

When the first grade marched out at the end of that day, Deborah threw me a look that said, "Help!" But at that moment I was completely occupied.

Ever since Miss Wilson found out that I can play the piano by ear, she has had me play for the marching out. It is all part of her campaign for bringing out my hidden virtues, I think. Usually I have to play corny old marches like "The Stars and Stripes Forever" or "The Burning of Rome." But I generally manage to sneak a little bit of rock 'n' roll beat under them when I can avoid Miss Wilson's eagle ear.

This day when I caught Deborah's look I went on playing, but I watched the first grade out of the corner of my eye. As the line broke up at the door, I saw some of the boys start toward Hannibal. But Hannibal didn't wait. He ran faster than I've ever seen a little boy run, but not as if he were scared. More as if he couldn't shake the dust of that school from his feet soon enough.

I waited till the fourth grade came marching by, and then I got Luella May Corbett to take my place on the piano stool. All she can play is "Barcarolle" and "Scarf Dance," but they would have to do today. And before Miss Wilson could notice that the music had changed, I hurried out the door to where Deborah was waiting, and she told me all about everything that had happened.

"Maybe I ought to go after him," I said, "before he does anything rasher."

"Take me along with you," said Deborah.

So I did, on my handlebars.

But we didn't see hide nor hair of Hannibal all the way to Silvermine Road. Even though he was new to that neighborhood, he must have found himself a shortcut through the woods, like a homing pigeon.

We stopped a few times and reconnoitered, but I still made pretty good time and we got to the red house way ahead of the school bus. Deborah climbed down from the bike and marched straight into the yard where the well is.

"If you ask *me*," she said. "What Hannibal needs is the magic. Come on, help me wish."

"Oh no, now," I said. "None of that."

Because that magic they talk about has always seemed pretty silly to me.

"Hadn't you better wait for the others?" I said. "They go in for that kind of thing more."

"No," said Deborah, "they've all got meetings. And anyway, they'd want to give advice and show me how, and it's my turn! I want to do it my way. But you're different. *I* can show *you*."

"Oh, dandy," I said. But of course I had to give in and humor her in her infant ignorance. "Well, all right, but make it snappy."

Only instead she made a big deal of it, putting me through all sorts of motions and making me repeat

all sorts of dopey words after her, because she said this was such an important wish she wanted to make sure it didn't go wrong.

"O well," I found myself saying. "O well, please help us help Hannibal to be good and get along with people and not be unhappy." And then she made me kneel down to the well and knock my head on the ground three times.

I felt ridiculous, because what if one of my gang passed by and saw? It would be risking my whole reputation. And then when I looked up I felt more ridiculous still, because somebody *was* seeing.

But I felt relieved, too, because the person looking at us was Hannibal.

But he was a different Hannibal from when I'd seen him last. His clothes were torn and dusty and his face was scratched by brambles, and he was panting as if he'd run all the breath out of him.

All the anger seemed to have gone out of him, too. And now that it had gone out, there was room for other feelings, and the greatest of these right now seemed to be curiosity. Because he was staring over the fence at us with big round eyes.

When he spoke, his voice was hoarse with dry-throatedness. "What you doing?" he said.

"Wishing," said Deborah, "on this well."

"Is that well *magic?*" said Hannibal, looking more round-eyed than ever.

"Yes," said Deborah, "it is."

"What you wishing?" said Hannibal, after a minute.

"We were wishing," said Deborah, "that the well would make you be good, and learn to get along with people."

I was afraid when he heard that, Hannibal might go wild again and start pushing everybody handy. I'll admit that's what *I* might have felt like doing if I were Hannibal and anybody said that to me.

But it seemed as though Deborah's wish must have already come true. About Hannibal's being good, I mean. Because he didn't say anything for a long time. When he did speak, it was in a small, ashamed-sounding voice.

"Can I wish, too?" he said.

"Sure," said Deborah.

Slowly and with dragging feet Hannibal came through the gate and up to the well. He looked at it, and then he leaned over and stared down it and muttered something. I don't think he meant us to hear what it was.

But I did hear.

What he said was, "I wish I were like other people."

I'll admit that when I heard that, my throat felt scratchy and as if I wanted to swallow. And for the second time that day I squatted down by Hannibal. I didn't worry about being butted in the stomach again, either.

"Look, kid," I said, "you don't want to wish a thing like that. You ought to be proud to be you. Why, you're the only one of you there is, just the way I'm the only one of me. There'll never be another person exactly like you ever again, anywhere in the world. So be yourself, dad, and like it!"

Hannibal stood looking at his feet and kicking the edge of the wellhead. "*I* like it all right," he said finally, "but *they* don't. If I'm myself, they won't want to play with me."

"They'll play with you all right," I said grimly. "They'll play with you or talk to *me!*"

Deborah nudged me and shook her head. And I saw that she was right again, and there had been enough crossness and fighting talk.

"You're all tired and dusty," she said to Hannibal.

"Don't you want to come inside and wash your face and have a drink of water?"

"*Me?*" said Hannibal. He looked down at himself. "I tore my pants," he added in a surprised voice. "My mom'll kill me."

"Maybe *my* mother can darn it," said Deborah.

"*Would* she?" said Hannibal, as if he didn't believe it.

"Let's go and ask," said Deborah. And she gave him her hand and they went into the house.

I stood looking after them. And suddenly I blew my nose. And then I remembered I was late for playing Kick the Can with the guys, and I got on my bike and rode away.

But the next day when I monitored at recess, I paid particular attention to what was happening over in the first-grade section of the playground.

It certainly looked as if Hannibal's wish had come true. There he was playing, just like the others. You wouldn't think he had ever felt different at all. And nobody seemed to be holding yesterday against him one bit.

Of course I heard later that Miss Silloway had lectured the class, after sending Hannibal out of the way on the pretense of a note to Mrs. Van Nest, and told the kids that Hannibal's first day had been hard on him and they should give him a second chance. And Deborah had specially asked all her friends to be nice to him, too.

Still, I'd say it would take more than that to make Hannibal suddenly fit in as well as he suddenly seemed to. I'd even say it would take magic.

And yet he hadn't stopped being himself, either. Because when I went near enough to make out the words, I heard him say, "If you think this teacher is strict, you ought to see ours on Lenox Avenue in New York City!"

And later on when he was in the middle of a game, he yelled out, "We don't play Prisoner's Base that way in New York City; we play it *this* way!"

I gave him a wink as I passed by. "How's yourself, dad?" I said.

"Okay, dad," said Hannibal. "How's yours?"

I have made Deborah and Hannibal promise never to let on to James and Laura and Lydia and Kip and Gordy how I wished on the well that day. And I must remember to cross out that part of the story before any one of them ever sees it.

Because I have always sworn to them that I don't believe a word of the magic, and I would no sooner go back on that than I would stop wearing my black leather jacket and my motorcycle boots. It is all part of the way I am, and if people don't like it, they can just lump it. A man has to be himself.

All the same, it is good to be a *little* bit like other people once in a while; at least, the other people that you like.

And so I am secretly glad that I have come part way round toward believing in the magic.

After all, if it weren't for *something* or other, I wouldn't even know Lydia and Deborah and the others. I'd still be moseying around with those drips Stinker and Smoko. And Hannibal wouldn't even have moved in, or if he had, he'd still be all miserable and fighting with everybody.

And what but magic could do all that?

So I guess I do believe in it, or sort of halfway. More or less. When I think about it.

But I will never tell.

7

James Joins In

I'm pretty sure I don't have to tell you who's writing this chapter.

Because all I can say is, who's left?

After all, if the magic were starting to comb the highways and byways looking for customers, it was time it remembered me, wasn't it?

Which is by way of saying that we all know about Dicky LeBaron's getting in on that last wish. Deborah tried, but she never *can* keep a secret.

If you ask me, Deborah's adventure was just about as good a turn to Dicky as it was to anyone else. He has improved a lot since. By seeing his own problems in the mirror of Hannibal, you might say. And by making friends with the well, as Laura puts it, instead of being so proud and superior and lone-wolfish about it.

We haven't let on that we know. About his giving

in to the magic, I mean. He still sneers about it in public, and we don't say a word. And he still wears that awful jacket and those boots, and comes swaggering over every so often and spends his afternoons with us maybe every day for a week. And then suddenly he isn't there, and stays away for ages, as if we didn't mean a thing in his young life.

It is his way of preserving his dignity, I think. And that is all right with us. But sometimes we have to laugh.

I would be the last to be jealous of Dicky LeBaron in any way.

I'll admit, though, that I felt sort of put out when I heard that the magic had welcomed him to its adventurous toils while I still hadn't had my turn. I realized the well was probably teaching me that I'm no more important than anyone else, even if I *am* the leader, usually. But still. There is such a thing as justice, isn't there?

But as time wore on, and October's bright blue weather gave way to November and bare trees and gray rain, I began to wonder if the magic had forgotten and were going to leave me out altogether.

And another thing happened. As the magic we'd already had slid farther and farther into the past, it began to seem less and less magical. To me, at least. To me it began to seem as though every single thing that had happened could have been accomplished by just goodness and thoughtfulness alone, without any well or any Hagar Gryce, either. And that was a discouraging idea.

Why, the summer before we'd at least seen a ghost, even if we weren't sure afterward we really had.

I began to hope that when and if the magic *did* remember me, it would do it in a really magic-like way and settle the question in my mind once and for all. And then it could forever afterward hold its peace.

And one night after supper I sneaked out in the yard all by myself and told all this to the well.

As to whether it heard or not, let the reader be the judge.

The Saturday after that dawned fair and cold. I forget who suggested that we take a long bike ride, but everybody agreed that it was just the weather for it, and we started out right after lunch.

Deborah was conspicuous by her absence. Dicky LeBaron had stopped by, and he and she were busy writing up the chapter of their adventure.

We headed north, which is always more adventurous. South just leads to civilization and the sun in your eyes. But north means hills and pinewoods and the end of suburbs and the beginning of real country, and tracking rivers to their source.

We have already done this with our own river. The first time we tried was way back in the summer, on the day we found the long-lost heir.

Since then we have done it hundreds of times, and we know now that our river comes tumbling down out of the reservoir, which is like the biggest and bluest of lakes, and we have discussed how maddening it must be to live on the lake's edge, as some do, and yet not be able to swim in it for fear of polluting the water company.

But today we went past the long-lost heir's house and beyond the reservoir, into undiscovered country.

"This is keen," said Kip, sniffing the high hilly air. The land all around us was wild and untrammeled, haunted by birch and laurel and with only a house or two every now and then to mar its utter north-woodsiness.

Then, in the middle of nowhere, we came on a fork in the road and a signpost. The arrow pointing one way read, "To Bald Hill." The other said, "Journey's End Road."

There is always something mysterious and romantic about a lonely signpost, with its promise of strangeness round the corner. Think of all the signposts in the Oz books alone and where they have led the fortunate reader!

And this one proved no exception to the rule.

"Which way'll we try?" said Gordy.

I was for Bald Hill myself. It sounded rugged and pioneerish, and like a place where you might meet Uncas, the last of the Mohicans. But the girls were curious about Journey's End Road and the kind of people who would choose to live on a road with a name like that.

"Did you ever hear of anything so utterly feeble?" said Lydia. "As though a person were perfectly ready to settle down and never have a single thing happen to him again!"

"Prob'ly sweet little old couples in little old cottages who're tired of it all," agreed Laura.

"Waiting for life's sunset with a tear in the eye of them and a smile in the heart of them." Kip giggled.

We had walked our bicycles down the road a little way as we talked. Now as we rounded a bend and saw the one house that seemed to be all of Journey's End Road, we broke off and stared.

What we were looking at was no cottage.

We had seen rich mansions before, but they were mainly either like the heir's house, all modern and glass and pink stucco, or like Mrs. Witherspoon's, with pillars and pergolas and porte cocheres.

This house was simply and to put it mildly a castle.

There were towers and battlements and buttresses. There was a moat with what looked like swans sailing on it, though when we came closer, these proved to be geese. There were tall turret windows with balconies under them, all just like a page out of Sir Walter Scott, as Lydia said.

"Or a picture in a fairy-tale book!" breathed Laura.

And suddenly I remembered my wish on the well that the magic would come to me in a magic-like guise.

Then, even as I remembered and even as we watched, a figure stepped from one of the tower windows onto the adjoining balcony. The figure was female and its dress was blue. Waving blond hair framed its enviable face. It stood scanning the horizon.

"It *is* like a fairy tale! 'Sister Anne, sister Anne, what do you see?'" murmured Laura, entranced.

What the girl on the balcony saw at that moment

was us. She waved a lily-white hand and her voice rang on the breeze.

"You, there! Boy!" were her words.

There were three of us who were boys, and Gordy and Kip and I all started forward, and then stopped and looked at each other.

"No, *you*. The good-looking one," said the girl.

It is the mere truth that I am taller than Kip and not so toothy as Gordy. But only a fatuous boob would answer to a remark like that. I swear I didn't move an inch. It was the others who pushed me.

Then, as I stumbled forward, staring up at the girl on the balcony and feeling my face get red, I knew that the well had not only granted my wish. It had done something more.

So far as girls were concerned, up till then they had always seemed more or less just human beings to me. If incomprehensible at times. And Laura and Lydia are not even too bad to look at.

But till that moment I had never understood what all the shouting was for in the love parts of stories and movies. Nor what all the poets were talking about, either.

But now, as I met the blue-eyed gaze of the yellow-haired girl on the balcony, something new happened. My head suddenly felt light, and my insides seemed to go all soft and warm, like melted ice cream. And I knew I would never be the same mindless boy, laughing in my happy carefree ignorant childishness again. I knew the magic had brought me to the parting of the ways where brook and river meet, and that I had become a man.

Words failed me.

"Hello," I managed to gasp out. "Were you talking to me?"

"Yes," said the yellow-haired girl. "I was. Help me down from here. I'm locked in."

"Princesses locked in towers!" cried Laura enthusiastically. "I *knew* this was going to be an adventure! Is a wicked ogre holding you prisoner? Does he beat you and feed you on bread and water?"

"Why, yes," said the yellow-haired girl. "That's exactly what he does!" And then she clasped her hands and looked straight at me. "Save me, gallant knight!" she cried. "Take me with you on your noble steed before the wicked ogre returns!"

Of course I knew it couldn't be like that, not really. There are no wicked ogres in this part of Connecticut. Still, I had wished for the magic to be really magic-like, hadn't I? And the well could have imported one, couldn't it? Maybe in a modern version.

"All right," I said.

But as I studied the castle, I wasn't sure how I was going to do it. Roses wreathed the stones of the tower romantically, but their stems looked frail for climbing, and thorny besides. And the girl's hair, while ample and suitably golden, was not of Rapunzel length.

"Just a minute," I said. "I'll think of something."

"There's a ladder in the barn," said the girl, rather impatiently, I thought. "Hurry!"

I ran for the barn. Kip and Gordy ran, too, which I thought rather pushing of them at the time. But I was glad of their help when I saw how big and heavy the ladder was. Together we managed to get it braced against the tower, and they held it while I climbed.

The long willowy tangly canes of the roses kept nodding picturesquely in my way, and their thorns were every bit as sharp as I had thought they would be. But I reached the balcony safely, if not unscathed.

Of course the proper way to rescue a Princess in a tower is to carry her down. But this particular Princess did not seem to want to be carried.

"I can climb by myself, silly," she said. "I'll go first and you steady the ladder."

It was awkward, scrooching to one side and sort of hanging in space while the beauteous maiden went past me, and I wondered how the fellows in the fairy tales managed that kind of thing gracefully. It was then that I tore the seat of my blue jeans on a particularly large thorn, too.

But the fair damsel proved nimble, and two seconds later she was poised lightly on terra firma. I jumped down the rest of the way and landed beside her.

Now that we were on the same level, I was surprised at what a big girl she turned out to be, nearly a head taller than I was. But that didn't make her any less beautiful. It just made me more humbly and devotedly her slave than ever.

And after all, Napoleon was a small man!

"There," said the girl, dusting off her diaphanous draperies. "Now then. I've got to get into town. Quick!"

"A matter of life and death, I suppose?" said Laura delightedly.

"Why, yes," said the girl. "That's exactly what it

is. I've got to get the important papers to the police before the gang of international spies gets back."

It seemed to me she had switched stories in the middle of the stream, but I didn't worry much about that at the time. I guess maybe I wasn't thinking very clearly about anything just then. All I wanted to do was lay my heart at her feet, and anything else I happened to have handy that she might care to trample on.

But all I could offer at the moment was my noble steed, or in other words the handlebars of my bike.

"Hop on," I said. And she did, and we started back in the direction of town.

But nothing had escaped the lynx-eyed ears of Lydia, and now she came pedaling up abreast of us. "I thought you said before it was ogres," she said suspiciously. "Now you say it's spies. Which is it?"

"It's both," said the girl. "I call them ogres cause that's the way they act, but they're really a dastardly spy ring. Hurry!"

This last was to me, and I biked harder. But Gordy put on a spurt of speed and came up on our other side and stared at the golden-haired girl curiously.

"Don't I know you from somewhere?" he said.

"I've never seen you before in my life," said the girl, not as if she ever cared to see him again, either.

"Yes, you have," pursued Gordy. "I remember you now, from dancing school. You were in the big girls' aesthetic group. You did the Dying Swan. Your name's Muriel Breitenwisher."

"Oh, that," said the girl. "They call me that, but it's not my name. I'm really adopted."

"By *spies?*" said Lydia incredulously.

"That's right," said the girl. "They stole me away when I was a baby."

"From your rightful kingdom, I suppose," said Laura, who had speeded up to join us.

"That's right," said the girl. "That's what the important papers are about. They're my claim to the throne. Hurry!"

This was to me again, and I tried to go even faster. But I was pedaling for two, and she was no light weight on the handlebars. Then, too, we'd already had a long pull from the red house up the whole valley to Journey's End Road, and the backs of my knees ached. Still, I was stronger than Gordy and in better training than Kip, and we gradually drew ahead of them.

But the doughty Lydia and Laura were still breathing hot on our heels, and now I heard them discussing the situation.

"Do you really believe she's a princess? I don't," said Lydia. "Do you think she's such a raving, tearing beauty? I don't."

"She does look awfully *old,*" admitted Laura.

"Not a day under fifteen, if you ask *me,*" said Lydia.

The yellow-haired girl could hear all this just as clearly as I could, and she did not appear amused.

"Do we have to waste time with these small fry?" she murmured.

Of course I should have stuck up for my friends. But I didn't. I was bedazzled by her azure gaze.

So I said traitorously, "Wait a minute and I'll get rid of them. Hang on tight."

For I had an idea.

Just ahead of us was a spot where they were fixing a hole in Valley Road. The men had quit work for the weekend and left the road closed off with parked trucks and planks and sawhorses. On our way from the red house we had had to get off our bikes and walk them around.

But I thought I remembered a space between two

of the sawhorses, and a rim of still unbroken pavement on the edge of the hole that would be wide enough for a bicycle wheel.

And sure enough, as the blocked-off piece of road came into view ahead, it was just as I'd pictured it. I didn't think any of the others could steer well enough to take the chance, but I was pretty certain I could.

"Now," I said.

"Eek!" shrieked the yellow-haired girl, shutting her eyes.

But we flashed through without joggling a single plank of the barricade.

I looked back in time to see the others skidding to a halt and dismounting. By the time they walked their bikes around, they would be too far behind ever to catch up.

I was alone with the beauteous maiden on the broad highway.

"There," I said.

But I couldn't think of anything more to say after that. I asked myself what Sir Lancelot would do in a case like this, or D'Artagnan, but that wasn't a bit of help.

The books tell all about knights and musketeers rescuing beautiful damsels. But they never put in what Lancelot said to Elaine on the ride home. Or D'Artagnan to Milady de Winter, either.

Maybe the idea is that just simply riding along with your fair lady on your pillion (or handlebars) is supposed to be enough.

I tried to think that it was.

But it was hard holding the thought on the last long hill into town. My legs were just about giving out, and all the yellow-haired girl said was "Hurry!" every other minute.

At the top of the hill I started to turn to the right.

"Where're you going?" she said.

"Town Hall," I told her, surprised. "You want to get those papers to the police, don't you?"

"Wait. Better scout around first. We may be followed. Turn the other way."

So we went to the left, down Main Street.

"Turn again here," she said, at the corner of Elm. So I did, and we wobbled slowly along dodging the umbrageous traffic while the yellow-haired girl glanced mysteriously this way and that, as a fleeing heroine should.

Our town on a Saturday afternoon is generally jammed with just about everybody shopping for the weekend and stopping to say hello to just about everybody else. I don't know how the yellow-haired girl could spot any lurking treasonous spies in that mob, but apparently she could.

For she suddenly said, "I was right. We *are* being followed. Quick. Stop here. Never mind the bicycle. Come on. We can lose ourselves in the crowd."

She had already jumped off and was getting in the lineup at the box office of the town's one movie theater.

What was playing was Moose Hardtop in a torrid love drama called "Branded Souls," and under any other circumstances wild horses couldn't have dragged me to see it.

But a darkened, crowded movie theater *would* be a good place to hide, though expensive. I would be alone in the romantic darkness with the beauteous maiden, too.

So I left my bike recklessly abandoned at the curb and dug in my pockets for what cash I had, and managed to scrape together enough for two tickets by owing three cents to the box office lady, who is an old and trusting friend.

The last thing I saw before we went through the door was Laura and Lydia and Gordy and Kip, pedaling madly up in front of the movie theater and then stopping short with baffled expressions as they saw us start inside.

I would like to say that I felt remorse at this sight, but I didn't. I was too busy thinking about the yellow-haired girl.

I did not notice any spies.

I followed the beauteous maiden through the door and handed our tickets to the man. Blinking in the sudden half-darkness of the inside lobby, I turned to my companion with an airy word.

And then I blinked some more, for another reason.

Someone was already there before me.

A lanky, flat-chested teenager with a ducktail haircut had materialized out of the shadows and was clutching the yellow-haired girl's hand in his hot, damp palm. I knew his palm would be hot and damp because I knew the boy. His name is Harold Tillinghast, and I could not despise him more.

"Muriel, baby! You got here after all!" he was saying.

"Didn't I tell you I would?" said the yellow-haired girl, now revealed in her true false colors. "Papa locked me in, but I told you I'd get away somehow.

This little boy helped me," she went on, adding insult to injury.

"Why, you!" were the words that rose to my lips as light dawned.

"Thanks a lot," said the girl brazenly. And she took Harold Tillinghast's arm and they went down the aisle together and sat in the front row and held hands. I know they held hands because I followed them. I was so stunned it was all I could think of to do.

And then I realized, and hurried back up the aisle for fear they would think I cared.

I stood irresolutely in the back of the theater as the dread truth went on sinking in. It was all a snare and a delusion. The yellow-haired girl wasn't a princess or adopted; she was just Muriel Breitenwisher. And there weren't any spies. It was all just a trick so she could get to the movies and meet Harold Tillinghast.

I stood there facing these humiliating facts. And I knew how Kay in *The Snow Queen* must have felt after the ice had entered his heart.

I saw Muriel Breitenwisher in all her utter baseness, a fickle flirt who would toy with a man and then cast him aside like an empty rind. And I knew that what was true of Muriel was probably just as true

of any other girl and that I would never trust wom-
ankind again.

Not only that, but it had cost me a dollar and sev-
enty-seven cents, not counting the three pennies I
still owed the box-office lady.

Not only that, but Muriel Breitenwisher had
called me a little boy.

I had half a mind to march right down the aisle to
where she sat, and demand my money back. But that
would be stooping.

And I didn't dare go outside, because Laura and
Kip and Gordy and Lydia would be there waiting,
and want to know all about it, and the thought of
telling them the truth, and the questions they would
ask, was too shaming to contemplate.

I stood there, while on the screen the mile-high
face of Moose Hardtop bent over the mile-high face
of Trillium O'Toole and murmured sweet nothings
in her ear, and for a minute it all got to be too much,
and I almost forgot I was a man.

But I pulled myself together and went downstairs
to the lounge, where the gum machines and pinball
games are.

Of course I didn't have any money left, but

I pulled all the handles in hopes that an unplayed nickel might be lying in wait, and even pushed the coin-return button on the pay telephone, just in case. But to no avail.

It seemed as if everything were against me. And the worst part was trying to figure out why the magic had done it.

I supposed, now it had made a man of me, it figured it might as well teach me to know a man's sorrows as well as a man's joy, but it seemed to me it was teaching me the hard way. I know that hard knocks are supposed to be maturing, but I have also heard of people who have grown up too fast, and it seemed to me the magic had made that happen to me. Spiritually, I mean.

I sat down in a chair and stared at the nearest gum machine.

And it was then, with hope at its lowest ebb and without even the solace of a comforting Chiclet, that I smelled the menacing smell.

I couldn't think what it was, at first. I had lived in the country too long. Out where our house is we do our cooking by electricity and there are no gas mains. But there are some in town.

And I had lived in New York City where our stove had a pilot light, and I knew what the smell of escaping gas is like. And now I remembered.

I sniffed the air and followed my nose, and it seemed to me the smell was strongest at the place where the floor and the outside wall met. It seemed to me I could hear a hissing sound, too, but I didn't wait to make sure. I went up the stairs three at a time and ran to tell the ticket-taking man.

At first he didn't believe me, but I kept talking till he started for the lounge to look for himself. Then I went racing down the aisle.

The magic had sent me to rescue the yellow-haired girl, and now that there was actual danger, I was going to rescue her whether she liked it or not.

She and Harold Tillinghast were sitting slumped down in their seats, and his arm was round the back of her chair. But I went right up to them and grabbed her by the hand.

"Come on!" I said.

"Well, really!" said the yellow-haired girl.

"Hey!" said Harold Tillinghast.

"Shush!" said the audience of enraged movie-lovers.

But I pulled her out of her seat (and away from

Harold Tillinghast's encroaching arm) and started dragging her toward the exit door.

"Let me go!" she said.

"No," I said.

She pulled back, but I was stronger (though smaller) and kept pressing onward. A second later we burst through the door and out into the un-noxious air of Elm Street.

"Let me go!" the yellow-haired girl said again.

"All right, I will now," I said. I dropped her hand and turned to leave, but a much heavier hand fell sternly on my shoulder and a voice said, "Oh no, you don't!"

I looked up and saw the angriest fat man (or the fattest angry man) I had ever seen in my life.

"So I found you!" he said.

"Hello, Papa," said the yellow-haired girl.

And I knew the fat man could only be Mr. Breitenwisher. He didn't look like an ogre, or a spy either. Chiefly he looked like an angry father.

"So you're Harold Tillinghast," he said, raking me with a contemptuous look.

"No, I'm not," I said. For there was no one I would less rather be.

"Humph!" he said, not heeding. "A pretty poor

specimen, I must say! Haven't I told you to stay away from my daughter?"

"No, you haven't," I said, but he wasn't listening. He was glaring at the yellow-haired girl.

"Muriel Breitenwisher, you come here to me," he said. "I'll teach you to go to the movies behind my back with Harold Tillinghast when we get home!" he went on, more forcefully than clearly. He turned back to me. "As for *you,* Harold Tillinghast, I'll teach you to kidnap my daughter!"

"I didn't," I said. "I wouldn't for anything." I was sorry now I had ever *seen* his daughter.

"Don't try to deny it," said the enraged parent. "With the guilty evidence right there on you for all to see! Does this fit the hole in your trousers or not?" And he waved in my face the piece of torn blue jean that I had last seen abandoned among the roseate thorns of the tower.

"It's circumstantial evidence," I said. "I can explain everything."

"You'll explain to the police," said Mr. Breitenwisher. "You'll explain to juvenile court!"

Out of the corner of my eye I had seen Laura and Lydia and Kip and Gordy, huddled in a group nearby and listening round-eyed to the scene.

Now Laura sprang forward to my defense, and the others followed. It was good of them, particularly after the way I'd been acting to *them*, but I wished they wouldn't. It just added to the mortification of the moment.

"You leave my brother alone," Laura cried indignantly. "All he did was save the Princess from your ogre-ishness!"

"What?" said Mr. Breitenwisher.

"Why did you adopt her in the first place, just to shut her in a tower and feed her bread and water?" said Gordy.

"I didn't," said Mr. Breitenwisher.

"All they were doing was taking the important papers to the police," said Kip.

"What papers?" said Mr. Breitenwisher.

"So she could get her rightful throne back from you international spies," said Lydia.

"One moment," said Mr. Breitenwisher. He bent an eye on his golden-haired offspring. "Muriel, have you been telling fibs again?"

"Oh, Papa," said Muriel. "It was all a joke. These little kids would believe anything!"

"Well!" was all Laura and Lydia and Gordy and Kip could say. I think they might have said more and

told Muriel what they thought of her, but at that moment there was an interruption.

Because at that moment the whole theaterful of people came tearing out of the front doors and the emergency exits, too, babbling with alarm and excitement and swirling about on the sidewalk. And the police emergency squad arrived, and the Volunteer Fire Brigade.

"What's happened?" everyone was asking.

"It's a tornado," said somebody.

"It's the dam burst," said somebody else.

"It's a bomb," said a third voice. "It's international spies. I heard somebody say so!"

I saw Harold Tillinghast skulking among the perturbed movie fans. When his eye fell on me and Mr. Breitenwisher, he turned tail and disappeared like the craven coward I have always known him to be. I could have pointed an accusing finger and explained everything, but I did not say a word.

And I couldn't have moved to point a finger, anyway. We stood hemmed in by the crowd, jammed uncomfortably close together and jostled by the people who milled around us, those who were trying to get out and those who were trying to get in.

Mr. Breitenwisher plucked at the sleeve of a policeman who was squeezing past. "Officer," he said, "I wish to report a kidnapping."

"Step to one side, please," said the policeman. "You'll have to wait your turn. We've got escaping gas here." And he pushed through and into the theater.

"What?" said Mr. Breitenwisher. "You mean my Muriel's life was in danger?"

"Yes, and this boy here saved her," said a voice.

And the ticket-taking man suddenly wormed through the crowd and clapped me on the back.

"That was some job you did, sonny," he said. He turned and addressed those who were standing near. "This boy here gave the alarm and saved everybody in the nick of time. But he saved this gentleman's little girl first. I guess he'll be the town hero from today on!"

"What?" said Mr. Breitenwisher again. "Do you mean to stand there and tell me Harold Tillinghast did a thing like that?"

I had had about enough. "My name," I said, as loud as I could, "is James Alexander Martin."

"Address?" said a little man with a notebook, bobbing up at that moment by my other elbow. I found out afterwards he was a reporter from the town newspaper.

"Silvermine Road," chorused Laura and Lydia and Kip and Gordy proudly. And the little man wrote it down.

"Some mistake here," muttered Mr. Breitenwisher. He turned to Muriel. "Thought it was Harold Tillinghast you wanted to go out with. Boy with a bad reputation. So they tell me. Not like this boy here. James Alexander Martin. Fine upstanding boy. Good-looking specimen. Go out with him any time you like."

He turned back to me and held out his hand. "Glad to know you, boy," he said. "Saved my Muriel's life. Eternally grateful. Feel free to take her to the movies any day in the week."

"Thanks," I said, vowing privately that I would not take Muriel Breitenwisher to a cat's funeral if she were the last woman on earth.

After that more things happened.

First of all the police and the fire brigade found and tamed the gas leak, which turned out to be in the kitchen of the restaurant next door.

And then the reporter interviewed me, and lots

of my friends turned up in the crowd, plus about fifty strangers who wanted to shake my hand. And the photographer from the paper took my picture in three different poses.

"Get in the picture, Muriel," I heard Mr. Breitenwisher say. And the beauteous Muriel tripped willingly forward.

But I rolled my eyes at the others, and Laura and Kip and Lydia and Gordy understandingly crowded around and between us. When the picture came out in the *Advertiser* the next Friday, it said, "James Martin and Friends." And only a part of Muriel's face and some of her long golden hair showed.

All the chatter and interviewing and congratulations took ages, and it was nearly suppertime before we finally got away. And when we reached the red house, the news had already preceded us, via sundry telephoning friends, and I found my mother and father and Deborah and Dickey LeBaron (who had been pressed to stay) waiting in congratulatory mood. And we all had supper together.

All this was gratifying, in a way. You can't help but feel good when your father shakes your hand and says he's proud of you, and your mother looks at you and smiles and suddenly has tears in her eyes.

But I knew the credit really belonged to the well, and I said so.

The party broke up early, out of regard for the weary legs of the travelers. And I went to my room a mass of mixed emotions, as the books say.

It seemed to me my adventure proved the magic was real all right. All those things couldn't have just happened.

And the well had heard my wish, too. Because the magic could easily have arranged for me to find the gas leak without that long detour to the Breitenwishers' house first. But I had asked for magic-seeming magic; so I got a castle and a captive princess and a spy story thrown in.

Of course they weren't *really* magic, like ghosts and witches, but that was logical, too.

We were older now, and the time had come to put away childish things.

It was when I remembered that, and thought of Muriel Breitenwisher, that my spirits sank, and people's congratulations were as the taste of ashes.

What did it matter if I was everybody else's hero, when love was an idle dream and women were fickle deceivers, and Muriel Breitenwisher had pulled the wool over my eyes and called me a little boy?

I lay awake and brooded about this for a long time.

Yet every cloud has a lining, be it ever so silver.

In school that next Monday morning Mrs. Van Nest made me stand up in front of the class while she told everybody all about the adventure at the movie theater. And when recess came, a lot of the kids wanted to hear about it all over again.

It was then that I noticed Florence Squibb on the edge of the crowd, hanging back sort of shyly. And when the others had turned from me to a game of run-sheep-run, she came closer.

"I think it was just wonderful, what you did," she said.

"Oh, it was nothing," I said.

"No it wasn't. It was just wonderful," she said.

"Do you really think so?" I said.

"Yes, I do," she said.

I had known Florence Squibb ever since we first moved to the country, and never thought twice about her before. But now suddenly I saw that her eyes were as big and blue as Muriel Breitenwisher's, and her hair, while not golden, was a pleasing shade of brown.

A week ago I wouldn't have noticed a thing like

that, but I was a man now. And the magic had done that for me, too.

"Ahem," I said. "Would you like to go to the movies with me sometime?"

"Yes," she said, "I would."

And we went that very next Saturday afternoon. We are going this coming Saturday, too.

So now I guess you might say I have a girl, in a way. And I don't have as much time as I used to for the well, or magic, or secret meetings with Kip and Laura and Lydia and Gordy and Dicky LeBaron.

After school when I don't have football practice, I generally walk home with Florence Squibb and carry her books.

Sometimes I look back regretfully on the old happy carefree days of wishes, and magic planning, and Saturday walks in search of mysterious adventure.

But having a girl is a kind of magic, too.

And if you don't think this is true, all I can say is, wait till you have one yourself.

And you'll see.

8

Everybody Ends

This is Laura writing now. James got to begin this book; so it is only right that I should end it. But there will be a little bit from everybody else in this chapter, too.

After James's adventure we could just about tell that the magic was over, at least for a while. After all, everyone had had a wish. And Thanksgiving was coming, which seemed to put a logical end to it, somehow.

I had an idea about that. And I told my mother and she agreed that it was a good one. So we had a big Thanksgiving dinner at our house and invited Kip and Lydia and Gordy and Dicky LeBaron. I made the turkey stuffing and James mashed the potatoes.

Before dinner, while we were enjoying our cranberry juice cocktails and while our minds were still sharpened with hunger and before the glut set in, I passed this book around for each one to write down truly what he was most thankful for. I thought it would make just about the best ending the book could have.

I took people in the order in which their wishes had happened; so Gordy got the book first.

And from here on you can read what each one had to say.

This is Gordy, and I am thankful to have had a wish on the well all to myself. Last summer when the magic happened before, I didn't get one.

Not that last summer wasn't wonderful. And not that the well didn't do me a good turn in letting

me meet James and Laura and the others, and get to know them and start doing things with them.

I guess it is no secret how I feel about them; so I needn't be ashamed of putting it down here that the well gave me a chance of my own, and brought Doctor Emma Lovely across my path, and led me to Sylvia.

I am glad to have helped Sylvia, partly for her own sake, but even more for mine.

Because good as it is to know people you think are wonderful, it is good to have somebody think *you* are wonderful, too, once in a while.

And Sylvia seems to think I am as wonderful as I think James and Laura and Lydia and Kip are. And yes, Dicky LeBaron, too.

I know I am not wonderful, of course, but it is good to have somebody think I am.

And that is what I am thankful for.

And I guess that's all.

This is Laura again now, just to say that Madame Salvini and Mr. Adam Appledore were married in Mr. Chenoweth's church this last Saturday morning.

It was a simple but picturesque ceremony. Madame

Salvini wore her wedding costume from the second act of *Lucia*. She wanted to sing, "Oh Promise Me," but we explained to her that brides just don't sing at their own weddings.

Lots of the Well-Wishers were there, and Deborah was flower girl, and the only attendant. The flowers were late chrysanthemums from Madame Salvini's own garden, and Deborah says there wasn't a bug or a beetle on them.

And Mr. Appledore tells me their orchard is coming along fine.

This isn't what I'm most thankful for, and I'll be back once more to tell you what *is*. But I thought you'd like to know how that wish ended.

And now it's Lydia's turn.

This is Lydia.

I suppose I ought to point out all kinds of morals, and say that the lesson I learned that day I tried to get even with Dicky LeBaron struck deep into my very vitals, and made me a better girl.

And in a way that is true.

What I learned was not only that Dicky LeBaron can be a good friend in a crisis, but that when you get to know him, he is a lot of fun, too.

Lydia drawn by Looey

And I think it's a good thing we did get to know him, because what with the way James has faded out of the picture lately and spends all his time with Florence Squibb of all people, we need *somebody* with a little gumption around here.

Dicky doesn't come around all the time, but when he does, he and I are the leaders now. At least we are the venturesome ones. But we have Laura and Kip to be sensible, and Gordy and Deborah to be cautious and keep us from going too far.

The thing is, though, that when you like somebody as much as I like Dicky LeBaron now, you realize how much time you wasted in not getting to know the person sooner.

And that's what the magic taught me, and I'm glad.

But I won't say I'm not thankful the hornets stung Stinker and Smoko, too.

Because I am.

This is Kip writing now.

I really have the most to be thankful for, because the magic sent the biggest wish to me. To me and Deborah, that is. And Dicky LeBaron, too, I guess.

I'm happy to report that the new family seems to be getting along just fine. And their garden is the neatest on Silvermine Road. Though of course it'll be spring before we see it in its glory.

And another thing.

This year some people started a teen canteen in town, to give the high school kids a place to go for sandwiches and dancing on Saturday nights. And on

Saturday afternoons it's open to us sixth, seventh, and eighth graders.

There is a jukebox in the canteen, but there is a piano, too.

And the father of the new family has volunteered to give one Saturday night a month, and one Saturday afternoon, to the canteen. Because it turns out he can play pop just as well as he can classical.

Dicky LeBaron is good, but the father of the new family is tops. He can teach Dicky a thing or two, and sometimes he does. And when the two of them get together, playing four-handed, the place really rocks.

Last Saturday afternoon at the dance I heard a boy whose father was one of the Smugs on that first day say he didn't know how we'd have got along if the new family hadn't moved in.

So it just goes to show that people *can* live together if they try.

I'm just sorry some people don't try first, instead of getting excited and stirring up trouble.

But I think maybe the magic taught this town how true this is. And if I helped the magic do that, then that's what I'm thankful for.

And now the end of the story of the new family belongs to Deborah.

This is Deborah writing all by myself, and not with Dicky LeBaron or anybody.

Hannibal just got elected treasurer of the first grade.

Deborah
drawn by Sylvia

This is Dicky LeBaron.

I don't think I belong in this book by rights, not really being in the Well-Wishers' Club, but Laura said I should write something, and the book is her idea in the first place, so here goes.

I'm glad I got to know these kids. I always kind of wanted to, though I would never have said. That's why I used to watch them, well spy on them really. Some of the things they did looked pretty square and childish, and yet they seemed to have more fun than anybody.

I see now why they do. It's the way they look at things, as if anything could happen the next minute. And generally something does. If you want to call it believing in magic, okay, call it that.

I always thought they'd despise me for being poor. Not that they're so rich, but you don't have to have much to be richer than I am. But they don't think about things like that.

In some ways knowing them has changed me a lot. I've learned to like reading, which I used to think was a waste of time, and even doing good turns, which I used to think was corny. And Kip is getting me interested in classical music. You wouldn't think such a

Ducky le B.
drawn by Lydia

down-to-earth guy would have long-hair tastes, but he does.

Sometimes, though, a man doesn't feel like books, or good turns, or pretending, or Beethoven's Fifth Symphony. A man just wants to go play Kick the Can with the fellows in the vacant lot. Or listen to Elvis Presley.

And when I feel like that, that's what I go and do.

I always come back, though, in the end.

My motto still is, stay cool, dad. And be yourself. Only not too much so.

And now I'll pass this book on to James. That's if he can stop thinking about Florence Squibb long enough to write in it. Ha ha.

This is James.

I don't mind Dicky and his jokes. He just hasn't found out about life yet. Though sometimes I think he and Lydia are beginning to see the light.

But every time I think that, the next minute they begin pushing each other around, and scuffling, and insulting each other, and become utterly childish again.

Not that there's anything wrong with that, while you're young.

James drawn by Lydia
My chin isn't that big
James

In fact, if we're all giving thanks, I think I'd say a happy childhood is what I'm grateful for most.

It's been wonderful having the well, and the magic, and now that I'm moving on into adult life, it will always be something to look back to. And tell my own children about.

I believe a man should marry young and have as many children as possible.

Of course I realize I have a lot to go through before then. High school and college and finding my place in the economic structure and all that.

But I don't believe a man can start thinking about his responsibilities too early.

When I first knew Florence, I told her all about the magic, and the well. I thought she might want to join the club, and wish with us.

But she couldn't think of anything to wish for.

And in a way, I consider that a tribute to me.

I'll admit, though, that once in a while when Florence is busy after school, it is fun to sit around with Laura and Kip and the others, just like in the old days, and idly plan what we will do if the magic ever starts up again.

I don't think it's very likely that it will, though.

After all, we are all growing up now, and if the others don't realize this yet, they will sooner or later.

So I'm afraid that for us it is good-bye to the well, and the magic, too.

But I'm thankful to have had it, while it lasted.

This is Laura writing now, for the last time.

I am thankful for every single thing that has happened since we moved into the red house, for the well and the magic and the good turns we have managed to do, and all the new friends we have made.

But yesterday, with Thanksgiving Day already more than a week ago and fading into the dim past, I was sitting by the living-room fire reading this whole book over. And I couldn't help feeling sad, in a way.

James can be awfully stuffy at times, particularly since he has started going around with Florence

Laura drawn by *Lydie*

Squibb, but there is something in what he says, all the same.

We *are* growing older, and things *do* change.

And it stands to reason that the well has run out of wishes, at least for us.

After all, magic has come into our lives now twice, and I know how lucky that makes us. Some people never have any magic adventures at all. It would be greedy to hope for any more.

But I am not disbanding the Well-Wishers' Club. Not yet.

There will always be good turns to be done, no matter how grown-up we get. And if they grow less and less magical as time grows on, we can still try to keep doing them by ordinary means.

All the same, as I sat by the living-room fire

yesterday and thought of winter coming, and how wonderful the summer and fall had been and how quickly they had passed, and as I looked out at the bare trees and thought of how James has changed and how we hardly ever see him anymore and how pretty soon the others will probably start changing, too, I, couldn't help feeling sad, as I say. And rebellious at life, and the way it is.

Because I don't want things to change, or people, either. I want them to stay exactly the way they are.

That was how I felt yesterday.

But this morning I got up, and everything was different. There was frost on the ground but the sun was shining and squirrels were scolding, and on the gable over the wishing well a late-departing phoebe sat and wagged its tail.

I looked at the world, and suddenly I felt as if magic were surely going to happen any minute. I can't describe how that feeling feels, but if you have ever had magic adventures, as we have, you will know.

I couldn't think for a minute why I was smiling. But then I remembered. It wasn't magic that was in the air. It was something else.

Today is December first.

And Christmas is coming.

Edward Eager (1911–1964) worked primarily as a playwright and lyricist. It wasn't until 1951, while searching for books to read to his young son, Fritz, that he began writing children's stories. In each of his books he carefully acknowledges his indebtedness to E. Nesbit, whom he considered the best children's writer of all time—"so that any child who likes my books and doesn't know hers may be led back to the master of us all."